Becky's Secret Surprise

The
Twelve Candles Club

9610

Becky's Secret
Surprise

Elaine L. Schulte

BETHANY HOUSE PUBLISHERS
MINNEAPOLIS, MINNESOTA 55438

Cover illustration by Joe Nordstrom

Published in association with the literary agency of Alive
Communications, P.O. Box 49068, Colorado Springs, CO 80949.

Published by Bethany House Publishers
A Ministry of Bethany Fellowship, Inc.
11300 Hampshire Avenue South
Minneapolis, Minnesota 55438

Printed in the United States of America.

Library of Congress Cataloging-in-Publication Data

Schulte, Elaine L.
    Becky's secret surprise / by Elaine L. Schulte.
        p.   cm. — (The twelve candles club ; #12)
    Summary: Prayer helps Becky deal with the changes in her life,
including moving to a new house, getting used to a sullen stepbrother,
feeling left out of the Twelve Candles Club, and worrying about a
friend's interest in hypnotism.
    ISBN 1–55661–540–X (pbk.)
    [1. Christian life—Fiction. 2. Clubs—Fiction. 3. Stepfamilies—
Fiction.] I. Title. II. Series: Schulte, Elaine L. Twelve Candles
Club ; 12.
PZ7.S3867Bg   1997
[Fic]—dc21   97–21119
                                                            CIP
                                                             AC

Again, to my wonderful readers.

ELAINE L. SCHULTE is the well-known author of thirty-six novels for women and children. Over one million copies of her popular books have been sold. She received a Distinguished Alumna Award from Purdue University as well as numerous other awards for her work as an author. After living in various places, including several years in Europe, she and her husband make their home in Fallbrook, California, where she writes full time.

CHAPTER

1

"Slumber party! Slumber party!"

The excited voices exploded from behind the thick pine trees in the concrete street divider, and Becky Hamilton jumped up from the front porch swing.

"Slumber party!" the familiar voices called out again. Colorful T-shirts flashed through the greenery.

They rode through the opening in the street divider on their bikes—the other four members of the Twelve Candles Club: Tricia, Jess, Cara, and Melanie.

"Slumber party!" the TCCers yelled in perfect unison.

Becky rushed from the front porch to the long driveway. If only she felt excited about tonight's slumber party, too. Instead, it felt strange for her friends to come to her new stepfather's house—even though it was only a twenty-minute bike ride away from her old house in Santa Rosita Estates. Worse, she'd have to tell them bad news—for the third time this summer.

"Hey, guys!" she called out, trying to sound enthusiastic. She definitely wanted to show how hard she was trying to blend into her new family.

"Hey-hey!" they yelled. They all wore backpacks, and their bikes' racks clamped down on colorful sleeping bags.

"I thought you'd never get here!" she said.

It wasn't as if she'd left southern California, yet living here on Seaview Boulevard, clear across town, felt so strange that sometimes—like right now—she felt like crying.

Leading the way came Tricia Bennett, Becky's best friend since playpen days. Tricia pedaled into the driveway, her long, reddish-blond hair flying behind her. Out of breath, she gasped, "You don't live next door anymore. It takes a while to ride way over here."

"Don't remind me," Becky answered. "I'm missing my old house. I mean *really* missing it."

Tricia rolled her green eyes dramatically and braked her bike. "I'm sorry. Why don't I think before I spout off?"

"Usually you do," Becky answered. "Usually."

Jess McColl braked her bike beside them and hopped off, her cropped light brown hair still perfect. She was short and sturdy, a super gymnast. "Let's face it," she said, "sometimes dear old Tricia is too candid."

"True," Becky had to agree. "Although normally she's very careful."

Tricia acted in lots of church and community plays, but right now her grateful smile wasn't an act. "Thanks, Beck."

"Where do we put our bikes?" Jess asked, getting to the point.

"In the garage," Becky answered.

They probably feel strange here, too, she thought. *They'd been perfectly comfortable visiting my old house in Santa Rosita Estates. If only Mom's marriage hadn't changed everything. If only Dad hadn't been killed in the car accident two years ago— and by a drunken driver, no less.*

Next, Cara Hernandez rode up and hopped off her bike. She was dark-haired, brown-eyed, a little shy, and a good writer. "It's a great house, Becky," she said, looking around. "I like front porches . . . and weathered gray shakes on the outside walls, too. It's homey."

"Yeah, I guess," Becky replied with a glance at the house. "I just don't feel at home here."

Next came Melanie Lin, their newest regular TCC member, who'd once been a New York model. She walked her bike behind the others, her shiny black hair blowing around her shoulders. "I know what you mean about not feeling at home yet," Melanie said. "When we moved from New York, I thought I'd *never* feel like a Californian, but I sort of do now. At least you know your way around Santa Rosita. You'll get used to your new house after a while."

"I hope so," Becky answered. "I sure do hope so."

She led them down the steep concrete driveway to the three-car garage on the lower level, then nodded toward the middle garage door, which stood open. "Mom thought we should park the bikes in the garage tonight so we can lock them in."

"Good idea," Tricia said, walking her bike into the garage. "After our ordeal with that burglar this summer, I lock up everything, and I do mean everything."

"Me too," Becky answered.

"Hey, this house has three levels, counting the garage

down here," Jess observed, probably to change the subject since the burglar had been at her house. "It's sure different than most southern California houses."

"It's different than Santa Rosita Estates houses, all right," Becky replied. "This one slopes down in back because it's on the hillside."

I'll bet they're wondering about all the cars now, she thought. *After having only one beat-up car until recently, the driveway here probably looks like a parking lot: Mom's green Oldsmobile . . . Mr. B's navy Cadillac . . . his tan camping van . . . and two stepbrothers' old cars.*

"It's a good thing Mr. B has so much parking space," Becky remarked. She hoped they didn't think Mom had married Mr. B for his money, because she hadn't.

"Mr. B?" Melanie asked.

"That's what I call Mr. Bradshaw," Becky explained. She remembered that Melanie had just joined the club around the time of her mom's wedding. "He didn't think we'd want to call him Dad since we already have a dad in heaven. Anyhow, Amanda calls him Paw-paw since his name is Paul," she said, referring to her little sister. "I decided to call him 'Mr. B' just before the wedding."

"Makes sense," Melanie replied. "He seems nice."

"He's all right," Becky answered. "It's hard to get used to having three big brothers, though. A lot about moving here has been hard."

"You're not the only one with three older brothers," Jess said, "but I've had my whole life to get used to mine. For you, it's been—boom!—suddenly three older brothers!"

Becky let out a sigh. "Jonathan and Charlie are all right. Anyhow, they're going off to college next week." She added about her difficult sixteen-year-old stepbrother, "Only Quinn will be here."

Melanie parked her bike in the garage alongside the others. "Too bad he's not going off to college, too."

"You know it," Becky agreed. She felt like saying, *It's bad enough having to change houses and neighborhoods—and soon, schools—without having to put up with a really weird stepbrother like Quinn.*

Stepping from the garage, Tricia glanced around. "Is that the potting shed, where he's going to live?"

Becky glanced at the white front door beyond the three garages. "Yep. He's already moved in. It's nice, like a studio—beamed ceiling, brick floor, lots of windows. He has a little view of the ocean, too, through those trees."

Jess remarked, "At least he's not living in the house with that snake of his. What did he call him?"

"Julius Squeezer . . . who is no longer with us, thank goodness," Becky replied. "He hasn't been seen since he escaped from Mom and Mr. B's engagement party at the Llewellyns'. Let's hope that snake is gone forever."

"Is Quinn in his room now?" Cara asked.

Becky nodded. "Probably. He spends lots of time doing scientific stuff on his computer."

Tricia gave a doubtful laugh. "Maybe he says he's doing scientific stuff on it, but he's really in there playing computer games."

They all laughed, Becky with them.

"Yipes! We'd better be careful. If his windows are open, he might hear us. He hates me having a slumber party in *his house*, as he calls it. This morning he asked his father, 'You

11

mean we're having *five* squealing twelve-year-old girls here in *our* house?' "

"What did Mr. B say?" Tricia asked.

"That he'd encouraged me to have friends over. And that Quinn used to be a twelve-year-old, too . . . that he hadn't been sixteen forever."

"What did Quinn say to that?" Cara asked.

"He snapped, 'But I wasn't a *girl*. I was never a *girl*!' He made being a girl sound disgusting. He even asked if 'that black girl' was going to be here—you know, Lily Vanessa. Mr. B made him come to church last Sunday, so Quinn heard her sing. He knows she's a visiting TCC member when she's in town."

"Humph!" Tricia replied. "And humph again!"

Becky grabbed Cara's sleeping bag and then scooped up Melanie's. "Come on. We can go up these back steps since we're back here anyhow. Be careful, the white railings were just painted."

"Where's the Bradshaws' dog?" Tricia asked.

"Quinn keeps Bullwinkle down in his room, and I keep Lass up on the terrace by my room. Bullwinkle's a spotted terrier and sort of feisty. He doesn't like my old collie. About the only thing they have in common, besides being dogs, is they're both brown and white. But Lass is more of a cinnamon color."

As Becky and the other TCCers tromped up the steps, they admired the terrace off the kitchen and living room. "Main floor terrace," Becky told them. "At least that's what Mr. B calls it."

Tricia sniffed and closed her eyes. "Ummm . . . something smells delicious from the kitchen. Cheesy and toma-toey."

"Lasagna," Becky said. "Mom made lasagna." It did smell good enough to make her mouth water.

"Nice view," Jess remarked. "Hey, there's the Llewel-lyns' house next door. Do you see them often?"

"They've been out of town lots," Becky answered about the eccentric couple who the TCCers often worked for.

She led the way up the top steps, looking up above to the third-floor patio, which held white lounge chairs, a glass-topped umbrella table, and white planters with bright red geraniums.

Lass saw the TCCers and gave a weak "Woof." The old collie stood up slowly and wagged his tail at them.

"Good old Lass," Becky said.

"Look at him," Tricia remarked. "He remembers us."

"Why wouldn't he?" Becky asked. "We haven't been gone from the neighborhood that long."

Tricia let out a small "Oops. Sorry."

"It's okay," Becky answered, even though not much was *okay* about living here.

All of these changes in my life aren't fair, she thought. *And it isn't fair, what's going to happen next. . . .* She didn't even want to tell them.

After petting Lass, the TCCers stopped to admire the view. Tall pine, eucalyptus, and California pepper trees covered the downhill slopes, and in the distance, the late afternoon sunshine made the bright blue Pacific Ocean shimmer.

"It's like living in a big tree house up here," Jess said. "My mom says the people who built the earlier houses in

Santa Rosita got the best views, like this one."

"Being a realtor, she'd know," Melanie said.

Becky glanced out at the ocean with them. "Sometimes you can see ships off in the distance. None there now, though."

"It's a good place for spying," Cara remarked. "I can picture a spy story set here."

"Just like a writer," Jess laughed. "Who else would think up such a wild idea?"

They all laughed.

"Come on," Becky said. "Let's get your stuff in my room. We can sit out here later. In fact, we could eat snacks out here if we want to." She lowered her voice. "Oops, Quinn might overhear every word we say if we eat here."

"Let's not sit here, then," Tricia said.

They made their way inside through the glass-framed door, which led to the bedroom hallway. When they arrived at Becky's door, she wondered how they'd react to her room since it still felt strange to her.

"It's almost like your room in your old house!" Jess said.

Trying to see the room with their eyes, Becky said, "Gram asked me how I wanted it decorated, and I was so miserable then, I just blurted, 'I want my old room!' Anyhow, she tried to make this like my old room."

Probably her new life looked wonderful to them. If only they knew how much she hurt inside. . . .

"Did your gram ever make it like your old room!" Tricia remarked. "Only this room's bigger. Your old room was so nice, though, I can't blame you for wanting to duplicate it here. A good thing your gram's an interior decorator."

Becky had to admit that her room looked nice. Blue

carpeting . . . blue, white, and yellow accents. Gram called the beds "a corner group unit with drawers." They were actually white bunk beds, and the head of one slid under the other. Blue drawers below each bed held socks and undies and folded stuff.

Gram had sewn big yellow and white daisies on powder blue comforters, then made coordinating pillows with huge daisies and white eyelet edging. Like at the other house, she'd stenciled matching daisies here and there on the white walls. Bookshelves surrounded the white desk across the room. And behind the door was the full-length mirror with daisies stenciled around it.

"You've got a white wicker coffee table and chairs like mine," Tricia remarked. "And a matching nightstand, too!"

Becky nodded uneasily. "I hope you don't mind our copying your idea."

"No way!" Tricia replied. "Besides, lots of people use wicker."

"Gram thought the room looked too empty, so we bought them. She's making blue cushions for the chairs, with little yellow daisies sewn on the cushions."

"What's behind all those shutters?" Jess asked.

Becky strolled to the tall shutters, pulled two open, and managed a dramatic, "Ta-da!"

Bright sunshine burst into the room.

"You have an ocean view!" Tricia exclaimed. "A really nice ocean view! You could do a great painting of it!"

Becky smiled, since her view was the one thing she liked most about moving to Mr. B's house. Another was the planters of cheery red geraniums blooming outside on the terrace.

"I've painted the view already," she said. "Actually, I painted it with my shutters and windows in front of the trees and ocean. I didn't want to do just another ordinary ocean painting."

She wondered how her voice could sound so steady when her heart felt like breaking.

Jess said, "Quinn can come up the steps to the terrace. With your shutters open, he can look right into your room."

Becky nodded unhappily. No sense in telling them that's why she usually kept the shutters closed. "Put your stuff down anywhere," she said. "Just not on the pizza party invitations on my desk, please!"

Everyone laughed and Jess remarked, "I thought I smelled pepperoni."

"I'll open a window," Becky told them.

They knew she made lots of the pizza party invitations, which sold like crazy at Morelli's Pizza Parlor. Each one was a folded-in-half sheet of poster board with a big pizza drawn on the front and dried pepperoni slices glued on. Inside, she wrote Place, Date, and Time.

The TCCers had no more than stacked their backpacks and sleeping bags on the floor when Becky heard someone coming down the hallway.

Glancing out the door, she saw Amanda. "Hey, what are you doing here?" she asked her five-year-old sister.

Amanda hurried into the room, carrying a tray with raw veggies, corn chips, and small napkins. Excited, her eyes darted around at Becky's friends. She was cute with her brown hair and big blue eyes, and—worse—she knew it. "Mom told me to bring the tray up for you guys," she announced.

Becky thought she must look suspicious because Amanda added, "She really did tell me to bring them up to you! She did! I promise!"

"Thanks, Amanda," Becky said. She took the tray from her and carried it over to her new wicker coffee table. "I believe you. You probably begged to bring the tray up."

"I did not!" Amanda shot back. "I did not!"

"Okay, you didn't."

As her friends helped themselves to corn chips and the carrot and celery sticks, Becky saw her sister still standing in the doorway. "Thanks a lot," Becky said again. "You did it just right, Amanda. You can leave now."

Amanda said, "I have a question."

"What's your question?" Becky asked, helping herself to a corn chip.

Amanda rolled her big blue eyes thoughtfully. "I was just wondering if you're gonna do anything to Quinn tonight?"

"Amanda Elizabeth Hamilton!" Becky exclaimed. "Have you been eavesdropping?"

Amanda shook her head and answered in all innocence, "No, I was just listening."

The TCCers clapped their hands over their grins, and Becky almost choked on her corn chip, then had to look serious. "It's wrong for you to listen when others don't know it. That's what eavesdropping is. It's listening in without the speaker knowing."

Amanda lifted her shoulders. "I just wanted to know what you're gonna do to Quinn. I thought when it got dark, maybe you'd put on bed sheets and go by his windows to scare him."

"It's an idea!" Jess said, excited.

17

"It's an idea, all right," Becky replied, "but I'm not sure it's a good one. He'd figure out how to get even with us. He's always talking about getting revenge."

Amanda stood firmly in place. "I heard Quinn on the kitchen phone, and he's going to sabo—sabo—"

"Sabotage?" Cara suggested while Amanda struggled with the word. "Is that the word he used?"

Amanda nodded her head importantly, making her thick brown hair bob up and down. "That's it. He's going to sab'tage your slumber party. Does that mean ruin it?"

"Come on!" Becky protested.

"I'm telling the truth," Amanda insisted. "He wants to r-u-i-n your slumber party so we won't want to live here. He said he wants to get us out of *his* house."

"Did he say 'his house'?" Becky asked.

"That's what he said," Amanda answered. *"His house."*

Becky drew a breath. "Guess I'm not too surprised."

The idea of Quinn ruining her slumber party was bad enough, but it wasn't the worst of her troubles. She'd wait to tell the TCCers the latest bit of bad news at bedtime.

CHAPTER

2

*O*nce Amanda left the room, Becky closed the door. She stood there, a warning finger at her lips. "Talk, guys," she whispered at them.

"What about?" Jess whispered back.

"Something!" Becky answered. "Anything!"

Tricia sat down by the wicker table and remarked loudly, "I do love this room! I love the French doors out to the terrace and everything else about it." She added dramatically, "Oh, Becky, this room is you! It's definitely you!"

Jess must have realized that Amanda might be listening at the door because she added another "It's definitely you!"

Becky slapped a hand over her mouth to stop a burst of laughter. "Definitely me?"

Finally Cara and Melanie caught on and began to talk wildly about the room, too.

Becky waited a long time, then whipped open the door.

No one.

The hallway was empty.

"She's gone," Becky reported with relief. "I thought for sure we'd catch her snooping."

Jess plopped down on the floor and began her leg stretches. "Good try anyhow, Beck. I thought you might catch her, too."

"Actually, I'm surprised she wasn't there," Becky answered. "She's such a snoop."

"I think all little sisters and brothers must be snoops," Tricia said. "Mom says that's part of how they learn."

Becky joined the rest of them, sitting down at her new wicker coffee table and reaching for corn chips. "Guess there's not much we can do to change little sisters or brothers, is there?"

"Maybe," Melanie replied thoughtfully. "Maybe if we really put our minds to it, we can solve this problem of sisters and brothers—and stepbrothers—in the universe."

Melanie was the brainiest one of them, but they knew she was teasing and laughed at the idea.

Tricia drew a breath. "How do you suppose Quinn means to sabotage us here tonight?"

Becky shrugged. "Knowing him, he probably has something scary in mind. Let's just hope it's not another snake or a big, hairy tarantula like when he tried to scare Mom before the wedding. I have to take half of the blame for that, though, since I put him up to it."

They glanced out the French doors toward the terrace, thinking that Quinn might be watching them from outside. No sign of him, either. Only the chairs, table, lounges, and Lass resting on his old rug.

"Lass always barks at Quinn," Becky told them. "It's as if he doesn't trust him."

"Smart dog," Melanie replied.

"I have an idea," Jess said. "Do you have balloons?"

"Mom might have some left from my birthday party," Becky answered. "And I know just what you're thinking, too! Bombing him with water balloons like Tricia and I did to you and Cara!"

Jess raised her chin. "There's nothing like being prepared in case he does try something on us."

Becky explained to Melanie, "Before we knew you, the four of us had a . . . a disagreement, and when Cara and Jess came over to TP Tricia's yard that night, we threw water balloons at them."

"You didn't!" Melanie said.

"We did!" Becky answered. "We sure did."

"And we were drenched!" Cara put in. She still seemed embarrassed because the disagreement had been her half sister's fault. "It sounds like a very good idea to be prepared for Quinn."

"If we have any, the balloons should be in the pantry by the birthday candles, napkins, and stuff," Becky thought aloud. "I think we have the small ones for water balloons there, too. Remind me downstairs. Let's not talk about Quinn anymore."

Melanie raised a finger. "Auntie Ying-Ying let me bring the video of our cruise. Maybe we can watch it later."

"All right!" Becky exclaimed. "I guess we'll have to use the TV in Mr. B's den. The cruise still seems like a dream to me . . . and a little bit nightmarish when I remember some of it."

"Wish we had a video of that goat chasing us on Miss Ida's ranch, too. It hasn't been a dull summer," Cara added.

"It's been fun, but we've had lots of challenges," Tricia put in.

Becky could guess what her new challenges would be. Blending into her new family and the changes that came with it. A battle about it raged in her heart already—especially about the latest bad news.

Half an hour later, Amanda knocked on the door, then opened it. "Time for dinner," she announced importantly.

"Thanks," Becky answered. "We'll be down in a minute. You don't have to wait for us."

"Okay," Amanda said, disappointed. "Don't worry, I won't eaves-eavesdrop."

"Let's hope not!" Becky replied and got to her feet. "Little sisters!"

Tricia and Melanie nodded, and Cara said, "Believe me, they're better than *older* half sisters."

"Probably," Becky admitted. They all knew that Cara's half sister, Paige, was a huge headache.

As they trooped down the hallway steps, Becky told them, "We're eating in the breakfast room so we'll have a little privacy."

When they arrived downstairs, Amanda waited at the edge of the breakfast room. "You want me to help bring in the plates with lasagna? I already brought in your glasses with ice cubes and your salads and the big pitcher of lemonade—"

"Thanks, Amanda," Becky told her. "Thanks a lot for your help. I'll do the rest."

Amanda turned with a sudden huff and headed for the

back door. "Then I'll go outside. Mom and Paw-paw and Quinn and I are going to eat outside on the *main* terrace."

"Great," Becky replied. "See you."

She led her friends to the breakfast room's glass-topped table, which was surrounded by graceful white metal garden chairs. At least Mom had the kitchen radio on loud, so she hadn't heard Amanda being important—and upset.

"Whoa, look at the great decorations!" Melanie said, admiring the table.

"It's a Texas theme," Becky explained. She'd made colored construction paper placemats shaped like the state of Texas, and for a centerpiece used a tan cowboy hat with a "twig tree" growing out of it. Each place setting held a stuffed surprise.

"Look . . . what are these little stuffed animals?" Melanie asked. "Hey, they're wearing cowboy hats and bandannas!"

"They're armadillos," Becky explained. "Amanda's animal book says they're the only armored mammal in the United States."

"Armored?" Cara asked.

"You know, as in 'suit of armor,' " Becky replied. "They have lots of armadillos in Texas. Mr. B was there this week, and he thought you'd all enjoy little stuffed versions."

"What do armadillos do?" Melanie asked. "We never saw them in New York."

"Not in California, either," Becky replied. "Mr. B says they creep around at night and burrow into the ground. Their skin is charcoal gray-colored armor, definitely not fluffy fur like these."

"You mean hard, like lizard skin?" Melanie asked.

"Sort of, only harder, I think," Becky answered. "Any-how, now we each have a stuffed, furry armadillo."

"We get to keep them?" Cara asked.

"Yep," Becky answered. "Presents for you from Mr. B. And check out the pasta in your salads."

She decided not to tell them that Quinn thought giving stuffed armadillos for slumber party favors was stupid. But then, he thought having a slumber party at all—or anything else she did—was stupid.

"Whoa, each little pasta is in the shape of Texas, too!" Tricia exclaimed. "I can't believe it!"

"I didn't either at first," Becky answered. "Mr. B thought we'd like it."

They were still talking about the cowboy hat centerpiece when she said, "Have a seat, and I'll go get our dinners."

"I'll help carry in plates," Tricia said, following her.

Jess sat down at the table first. "And I'll pour the lemonade."

In the kitchen, Mom stood at the cooking island, serving huge chunks of lasagna on the white plates. Her long, dark hair had frizzled from cooking, but she hummed happily. Still, she seemed out of place in this kitchen.

"Tricia!" Mom said, looking up from the plates. "I've been missing you."

"Hi, Mrs. Hamilton . . . I mean, Mrs. Bradshaw."

Becky drew an unhappy breath. Tricia had known Mom practically all of her life, so it was going to be strange to call her something else.

Mom gave Tricia a hug. "It takes a while for people to get used to my new name. I'm not even used to it myself."

Becky didn't want to hear any more *getting-used-to* talk.

That's all she'd done ever since Mom and Mr. B had fallen in love. Best to change the subject. "Everyone thinks the little armadillos and the Texas-shaped pasta are great."

"They're original, all right," Mom agreed. "You know what Paul says about them—'Only in Texas!' "

Becky grabbed two plates and started for the breakfast room, hoping to avoid Amanda as she hurried inside through the back door.

"I'm helping to set *our* table," Amanda announced.

"Great," Becky told her. "Glad to hear it. I know you'll do a good job."

Amanda raised her chin and said in a huff, "I will. I'll do a great job."

Tricia carried in two plates, and Mom brought the last one into the breakfast room. "Hi, girls," she said. "I'm so glad you're here."

"We are, too, Mrs. . . . ummm . . . Bradshaw," Jess said.

Mom's new name is awkward for everyone, Becky thought. *Very awkward.*

After Mom had visited for a minute, she glanced at Becky as if to ask, "Have you told them yet?"

Becky sat down, pretending not to notice. No way was she going to tell them the news now.

"Well," Mom said, "I'd better get everyone else's dinners. We'll be outside."

Once she'd left, Tricia said grace, which wasn't surprising, since she was the strongest Christian of the group and the most used to praying aloud.

When Becky opened her eyes, she noticed that Cara had a curious expression on her face.

Hadn't Cara prayed with them?

Strange.

Jess whispered to Becky, "Don't forget the balloons."

Becky glanced into the kitchen. She couldn't see anyone from where she sat. Maybe Mom and Amanda were carrying food out to the terrace.

Tricia must have read her mind because she craned her neck to peer out the window. "Looks like everyone except Mr. B is out there now. The coast is clear."

"'Scuse me," Becky exclaimed, nearly knocking over her chair. She rushed to the kitchen, opened the pantry doors, and found a package of balloons by the birthday decorations. She grabbed it and quickly stuck the package inside the waistband of her shorts, closed the pantry doors, and rushed back to the breakfast room.

"Got 'em?" Tricia asked.

Becky nodded. "Got 'em." It seemed slightly wicked, but they'd only water-bomb Quinn *if* he came after them.

"Great," Jess said. "We're prepared."

Becky took a bite of lasagna. Delicious.

Just then Mr. B stuck his head into the breakfast room. "Hi, girls." His nice blue-gray eyes sparkled with friendliness. "Good to see you." His blond-gray hair and beard were perfectly trimmed, and he wore a neat yellow shirt and khaki pants, looking nice, as usual. He repeated his jovial "Good to see you."

The TCCers answered with a plain "Hi!"

They probably don't know if they should call him Mr. B or Mr. Bradshaw, Becky thought. Everything had become so complicated.

"I've never seen twigs grow out of a cowboy hat before," he remarked, eyeing the table decorations. "Doesn't

Becky's centerpiece look wonderful? She's so creative."

Becky felt herself blush, especially when everyone agreed.

Tricia told him, "Thanks a lot for the cute armadillos—"

"Yeah!" the others chimed in. "Thanks a lot!"

"My pleasure."

"Umm, Mr. B," Becky began, "Melanie brought the video her aunt took on the cruise. Can we . . . I mean, may we play it on your den TV?"

"Sure," he said. "Do you know how to use it?"

"I think so," she replied.

"Let me know if you need help." He hesitated. "Ah, I have a question for you girls. Ready?" When they nodded, he asked, "What did the ocean say to the shore?"

Another one of his jokes, Becky decided.

Everyone thought for a few moments, then Tricia shrugged. "We give up. What did the ocean say to the shore?"

Mr. B gave a laugh. "Nothing. The ocean just waved." He laughed more, making them laugh a little, too.

Amanda came running in, full of importance again. "Paw-paw! Paw-paw! Time for us to eat dinner!"

"If you girls will excuse me, it seems my dinner awaits, too. Have fun."

When the door closed behind him, Jess said, "He's nice. . . really nice."

Becky had to agree. "Yeah, he's okay."

"I forgot what he does," Jess said.

Becky forked up a Texas-shaped pasta from her salad. "He's a consultant, meaning he flies around the country to solve people's problems. He's partly retired, so he's around home a lot more than he's gone."

"Wish my dad were around more," Melanie said. "One thing about having a doctor for a dad, they're at work a lot."

Everyone was quiet for a while, then Tricia asked, "So how was registration at Ocean Middle School yesterday?"

Becky shrugged. "All right, I guess." She explained to Melanie, who probably didn't know. "It's a big old Spanish-style building in the older part of town, but it looks like everything's going to be all right."

"Are there gangs there?" Melanie asked with concern.

"I hope not!" Becky exclaimed. "I don't think so."

"Do you know any of the kids there?" Cara inquired.

"Only the ones from Sunday school class," Becky answered, her stomach feeling hollow. "Let's talk about anything else. Say, does anyone have new school clothes?"

She was glad to hear about their latest purchases. Melanie was really into clothes and knew what colors and styles made everyone look good and was glad to share it.

After they finished dinner, Becky asked, "Anyone want seconds?" No one did because the chunks of lasagna had been so huge. "How about dessert? We have vanilla ice cream and chocolate-covered pecans from Texas."

Jess laughed. "Where else? Giddy-up, cowboy! Let's try 'em. Bring on those chocolate-covered pecans, pardner!"

Laughing, they helped Becky clear the table and put the dishes into the dishwasher. That done, they carried spoons and cut-glass dessert dishes to the breakfast room.

"Nice dessert dishes," Jess remarked.

"They belonged to Mr. B," Becky told them. She'd almost said, *and his first wife*, who they knew died of cancer. She quickly added, "You guys are all right. We could probably get away with not cleaning up the dishes tonight."

Tricia put on a broad smiley face. "The Twelve Candles Club seeks to please. Our reputation is always at stake."

In the breakfast room, Becky scooped vanilla ice cream from the gallon container into the cut-glass dishes. "We're going to have to have a special meeting of the Twelve Candles Club tonight," she told them.

"Another meeting!" Tricia said. "What's it about?"

Becky took her time placing chocolate-covered pecans around the scoops of ice cream in each dish. "You'll find out. You'll find out in a while."

She definitely did not want to discuss it now. Instead, she prayed, *Lord, give me a good attitude about what I have to tell them.*

———

After dinner, they carried their little stuffed armadillos to Mr. B's den. Becky pulled the drapes shut to darken the room, then turned on the video. The first scene showed them tossing confetti in the air as their ship left port. The next scenes were action-filled, taking care of kids in the youth rooms. Next came pictures of them visiting Caribbean islands, then dressed as pirates for the passengers' Amateur Night.

"Ho, ho, ho!" Quinn laughed in a phony voice as he poked his head into the room. "Well, aren't you girls scary pirates? Everyone must have been terrified by your brilliant personifications of the privateers."

"Stop it, Quinn!" Becky said.

His tall, skinny shape made him look peculiar in the video's flickering light. His gold wire glasses gleamed, and he eyed Becky and the other TCCers suspiciously, as if they were trespassing in his father's den.

Definitely unfriendly, Becky thought.

Amanda peeked into the room behind him. "What's per-per-son-i-fi-cations of priv-a-teers?"

"Pretending to be pirates," Becky answered. She turned to Quinn. "Why don't you speak plain English?"

"Because there's nothing plain about me," he answered, raising his chin. " 'Plain' means simple, straightforward, unambiguous, understandable—"

"That's true, all right." Becky drew a breath. "You're none of those."

Bullwinkle, his spotted terrier, raced into the room, trying to lick everyone's faces.

"Down, Bullwinkle!" Becky ordered. "We don't need our faces washed with your tongue. Quinn, get him out of here!"

"Why should I?"

Becky's stomach tightened. "Because he's your dog, and my friends don't necessarily like having their faces licked—"

Just then Mr. B called from the kitchen, "Bullwinkle, dinner! Dinner!"

It was the one command Bullwinkle understood, and he bounded out of the room toward the kitchen.

If only Mr. B would call Quinn, Becky thought.

As a hint to him, too, she said to Amanda, "What did Mom tell you about not hanging out with us tonight?"

Amanda let out an indignant breath and trudged away.

Instead of taking the hint, Quinn asked, "Did you girls eat your stuffed armadillos?"

"Get real, Quinn!" Becky objected.

He shot her a smile, then spoke in his superior voice. "The American nine-banded armadillo is a native of South and Central America but is found as far north as Texas. It's America's only mammal protected by heavy, bony plates that cover its head, body, and tail. When the Spaniards first came to America, they called the armadillo 'little armored man.' "

"That's enough, Quinn," Becky protested.

"An armadillo can grow to three feet long," he continued. "For you girls, that means as long as a yardstick. Despite the armadillo's short legs, it can move with considerable speed. Its pointy snout, like an anteater's, can dig out insects and crayfish—"

"Quinn!" Mr. B called from the kitchen.

Quinn rolled his eyes and yelled back, "I was just explaining—"

"Quinn!" Mr. B interrupted. "Let's give the girls some space tonight, okay? How about giving me a hand outside?"

"Coming," Quinn replied unhappily. "I'm coming."

Thank goodness! Becky thought.

She turned with the other TCCers to watch the video again. The scenes were of their last day aboard the cruise ship. She felt the package of water balloons stuffed in her waistband. *If he comes around tonight trying to scare us, he'll deserve being drenched,* she told herself. *He'll deserve it. As if I didn't have enough troubles without him!*

CHAPTER

3

Upstairs, they set their stuffed armadillos in a careful circle on the wicker coffee table, then eyed her. Becky decided they seemed nervous, as if they suspected she had bad news about the club.

"The armadillos look like covered wagons circling the campfire," Jess remarked, breaking the silence.

"Only you'd think of that," Tricia said. "You with the California pioneer family."

"So true," Jess answered with a grin.

Everyone quieted, and Becky quickly pulled the package of balloons out from under her shorts' waistband. "Balloons! Water balloons! Come on, you guys!"

"We'll bomb Quinn if he comes around," Cara said. "Whoa, maybe I should stop being so nice to Paige and hit her with water balloons sometime. Can't you just see her having a fit over her hair being ruined?"

"I can," Becky said. "I definitely can."

"You wouldn't believe it," Cara added. "Paige is now into hypnosis."

"Hypnosis?!" Tricia repeated. "You're kidding."

"No, I'm not," Cara assured her. "Actually, it's sort of interesting. She thinks being hypnotized is great."

Becky glanced at Tricia, who opened her mouth to speak, then quickly closed it. Maybe it was one of those times when she felt God was telling her to keep her mouth shut.

Becky was on the verge of saying that the Bible spoke against hypnosis, psychics, witchcraft, and other kinds of spiritually dangerous stuff, but if Tricia didn't say it, maybe she shouldn't, either. Besides, she wasn't sure where to find it in the Bible.

"To the bathroom!" she announced, waving the package of balloons in the air. "Everyone to the bathroom to fill balloons with water!"

Talking and laughing, they trooped after her.

Once they were all in the bathroom, Tricia remarked, "Hey, it's a big bathroom, even with all of us in here. A great old bathroom. I really like it."

"I guess they made bathrooms bigger years ago," Becky replied. "I kinda like it, too."

She glanced around the mostly white bathroom with them. Old-fashioned brick-shaped white tiles surrounded the big tub, and tiny white octagonal tiles covered the floor. A huge pedestal sink stood under the mirror—definitely not like the kind of bathroom furnishings you found in Santa Rosita Estates. The latest addition, a new white balloon shade, hung at the window. So far, the only other colors were her blue towels and an old, tall blue vase with silk sun-flowers sprouting from it.

"The room needs more color," she told them. "More blue and yellow. And maybe some green plants, too, to carry out the green from the treetops outside the window."

"Great idea," Tricia said.

"Enough about decorating," Jess said, then got right to the point, as usual. "Which faucet should we use for filling the balloons?"

"Looks like the sink and bathtub faucets might both work," Becky decided. "I'll do the bathtub. Be careful—"

"It has real porcelain faucet handles," Cara remarked.

Tricia wiggled a red balloon up the metal spout of the faucet and turned on the water. "Yiii!" she squealed as cold water squirted all around. She turned off the water fast. "Uff, it sprayed the mirror!"

"Just towel it off," Becky told her. "In a bathroom with this much tile, a little extra water isn't such a big deal."

"Thank goodness," Tricia said, starting to wipe down the mirror. Suddenly she turned and, laughing, sprayed a spurt of water at them.

They all squealed, running for the door.

"You wacko!" Becky told Tricia. "We don't want to mop the whole room. Stop it, and I'll towel-dry the floor." She grabbed an old towel from a cabinet and began to wipe the floor dry.

Melanie gave a laugh as she stepped carefully back into the bathroom. "Yeah, Tricia, cool it! We don't have extra clothes with us for getting drenched. Just clothes for church tomorrow morning—"

"Only Model Melanie would be worrying about

clothes," Jess laughed. "Anyhow, you're not very wet."

Tricia stuck a limp balloon over the faucet. "This time I'm going to focus on getting the water *into* the balloon." Concentrating, she slowly filled a red balloon with water and handed it to Jess. "Ta-da!"

Jess tied it off. "One balloon complete. Where'll we put the filled balloons?"

Becky glanced around. "Let's keep them in the bathtub, over on the foot end. That way, we can pile them up there and I can still use this faucet."

She grabbed a blue balloon and wiggled it onto the bathtub faucet. "Hey, all right. This is working perfectly."

"I'll help Jess tie off balloons," Melanie offered, taking the bulging blue balloon from Becky. "But it'd be more fun to have a water battle right here and now."

"No way!" Becky answered, filling another balloon at the bathtub faucet. The truth was she felt like having a wild water battle, anything to get the anger out of her. She said, "Yellow balloon done in a second. . . ."

BANG! The balloon burst, splatting water all over her and the room.

She squealed with the others as the cold water hit. "O-o-o! I'm drenched!"

"I thought we weren't going to have a water battle!" Melanie said with a laugh.

"We weren't!" Becky answered. "We're not going to—"

That moment, Tricia's balloon burst at the sink.

"Yiii!" everyone screeched. "Another one!"

Tricia hooked her wet hair behind her ears. "Yellow balloons must be weaker than others."

Jess wiped water from her arms. "Impossible."

"Anyhow, no more yellow balloons," Becky said. "We'll be mopping up all night."

Melanie held her wet tee away from her middle. "When we're done, we'll have to get in our jammies. We can hang the wet stuff over plastic hangers on the shower curtain rod."

Jess laughed at Melanie. "Actually, the cold water feels good," Jess said.

"We just can't fill them too full," Becky said.

Finally, twelve colorful, bulging balloons lay in a huge pile in the bathtub. That done, Becky found enough plastic hangers for their wet clothes. "Let's change into our jammies."

Before long, their clothes hung over the shower curtain rod, and they wore their dry nightclothes. *The time to tell them the bad news is now*, Becky thought.

"Let's sit around the coffee table," she suggested. Once they sat down, a strange quiet fell over her room.

"So what's the big mystery?" Tricia asked. "Are we going to freeze each other's underwear or tell our deepest, darkest secrets?"

Becky shrugged. "I don't know about those—"

"You're going to make us go gawk into Quinn's room," Jess guessed. "Maybe even scare him!"

"No way!" Becky answered. "No way!"

"A secret—or a surprise—is going on, though," Tricia said. "Something is bothering you."

"How did you know?" Becky asked her.

"We haven't been friends all these years without my learning when something's bothering you," Tricia answered.

Becky drew a deep breath and looked down at the table's white woven wicker. No way could she look them in their faces now. No way!

"It's not easy to talk about," she began, "but I'm . . . going to have to tell you now or later." She gulped and made herself go on. "I have to give up being president of the Twelve Candles Club."

"Give up being president?!" they exclaimed.

Becky straightened her spine. "Mom and Mr. B think it's just too much for me to be driven over to Santa Rosita Estates after school every single day. I'd still do all of the jobs I've signed up for, do Morning Fun for Kids next week, too."

She tried to keep her voice light and easy—and not sounding sorry for herself—but her head began to ache and her throat felt tight. "After school starts, they thought maybe I could just come to meetings and activities once in a while," she managed to get out. "You know, like for washing cars on Saturday mornings."

"No way! Not after all of your work getting the club going!" Melanie exclaimed. "Just think of all the flyers you made, not to mention your TV and newspaper interviews after your wacko dog chase!"

Becky nodded. Her head began to throb as she remembered how the club had started. She'd prayed desperately that her family could earn enough money to stay in southern California, and when she'd blown out the twelve candles on her birthday cake, the idea had hit: a girls' working club to do baby-sitting, house-cleaning, pet-sitting, and even party-helping.

Now the other TCCers sat stunned.

"What about riding your bike to the meetings?" Cara suggested. "You could do that."

"I could until school starts next week. But it's already beginning to get darker earlier, and going off Daylight Savings Time will make it worse. They said they'd get me there on Fridays after school and for slumber parties."

Tricia groaned, shaking her head. "I can't believe it! I just can't believe it! You've been such a great president! This is going to ruin the whole club."

"It makes sense, though," Jess said. "We shouldn't be surprised now that Becky lives way over here. What we need to do is to figure out how we can get around this."

Tricia brightened. "I have an idea! You could stay at my house Friday nights, and we could wash cars Saturday mornings and do other weekend jobs—"

"And you could go back home to your family after church on Sundays," Jess interrupted. "In fact, we could take turns having you on Friday and Saturday nights."

"I'd like to," Cara offered. "I volunteer."

"Me too," Melanie said.

Becky felt just slightly better because she'd hoped they'd say something like that.

"You couldn't come to other meetings?" Melanie asked. "No other meetings at all?"

Becky shook her head. "Only Fridays after school," she answered. "Mom and Mr. B want us to make friends at our new school, too. They keep saying that life is full of changes, and we have to get used to change sooner or later." She couldn't help sighing. Too many changes!

"It makes sense," Jess said, "but it's sad."

"Very sad," Tricia agreed.

They quieted, and Becky took a big breath. She cleared her throat, seeing all the girls look at her with interest. "It probably won't surprise you to hear I've been giving this lots of thought. Jess might be vice-president, but she has gymnastics starting again. Right, Jess?"

"Right!" Jess answered emphatically. "Besides, I only promised to be vice-president in charge of the phone, photocopying, and using my room for meetings."

"Anyhow," Becky said, keeping her voice steady, "we have to have a special meeting now and vote for a new president. That's how we should go about it."

"Guess so," Jess said. "We have to do it whether we want to or not."

Becky hesitated, then panicked, wondering how she could get through this. She forced herself to say, "This special meeting of the Twelve Candles Club will now come to order. We will dispense with the secretary's and treasurer's reports, and with 'old business.' "

For an instant, she thought she'd cry, but a hard swallow overcame it. "The 'new business' tonight is the nominating and voting for a new president. Are there any nominations?"

The TCCers gazed unhappily at her.

She swallowed again. "Any nominations?"

They all shook their heads.

Becky took a deep breath. "Then I would like to nominate Melanie Lin for president. She's proven herself to be honest, capable, and hard-working for the Twelve Candles Club—"

"I can't do it as well as you can, Becky," Melanie protested. "Really, I can't. I've never been president of anything, and I'm just learning about baby-sitting—"

"I was never a president of anything before, either. And you did a great job on the cruise ship," Becky told her. "You have lots of patience with kids." *Besides*, Becky thought, *Melanie's modeling career isn't doing much since she moved here.*

A picture of their youth pastor, Ted Iddings—Bear, to the kids—came to mind. "You know how Bear is always telling us to discover who we are and how God has made us special. Well, I accepted the job because I was desperate to work then. But by doing it—by being president—it helped me to see that God can use me as a leader. I think you can be one, too," she told Melanie.

Melanie eyed her uneasily, and Becky rushed on. "I've thought about the others. Tricia is perfect as treasurer, and Cara is perfect as secretary. That leaves you."

Melanie glanced at Jess, Cara, and Tricia. "Don't any of you guys want to be president? Tricia, how about you?"

Tricia shook her head. "I've got a big part in a play coming up when school starts."

"Cara?" Melanie asked.

Cara's shyness seemed to overcome her. She shook her head. "No, thanks. I'm just not . . . ready for that."

Becky forced herself to go on. "Then does anyone second the nomination of Melanie Lin as president?"

"I second the nomination," Jess answered. "But we better be sure that Melanie is willing."

"Are you willing?" Becky asked her. "I sure hope so. We need to keep the club going. . . ."

Melanie rolled her eyes. "I'm willing to be willing, at least. Are you guys sure no one else wants it?"

The others shook their heads.

Becky drew a deep breath. "Well, then, the nomination

of Melanie Lin as president of the Twelve Candles Club has been seconded. All in favor, raise your right hands." Becky raised her hand quickly, trying to be businesslike.

Jess, Cara, and Tricia raised their right hands, and Melanie just pressed her lips together.

"Vote, Melanie," Jess told her.

"Oh, all right," Melanie said and raised her hand, too.

Becky announced, "By unanimous vote, Melanie Lin is now president of the Twelve Candles Club. Congratulations!"

"Yeah, congratulations!" the others called out.

With everyone talking to Melanie, it was easier for Becky to press her lips together to keep from crying. By the time they turned back to her, she had her emotions under better control.

"Hurray for Melanie!" Jess exclaimed.

"And thanks to Becky!" Cara said.

"Listen, guys," Becky said. "I'm not quitting the club completely. I'm not going to, that's all!"

"That's good news," Tricia answered and gave Becky a hug. "After what we've all been through this summer, we're always going to be friends. Always and forever. Remember that, guys. We're always going to be friends, no matter what we do in life or where we live."

Becky swallowed harder. Friends help friends heal their hurts, and even though giving up being president hurt now, she wouldn't trade the TCCers for anything.

By the time the special TCC meeting ended, darkness had fallen. Only dim lights from distant houses below lit the night beyond the terrace windows. Although normally she'd have closed her shutters, with so many people in her room, she felt safe with the shutters open.

She got up and grabbed her art tablet and a pencil from her desk and took them to the wicker coffee table. The TCCers were talking about school and messing with their stuffed armadillos. Maybe she'd draw something to depict each one of her friends. She began to sketch

parallel bars for Jess . . .

a pad and pen for writer Cara . . .

an Oscar award for Tricia . . .

a book balanced on top of her head for Melanie . . .

a nicely shaped head with corn-row braids and musical notes flowing from her mouth for their new, whenever-she-was-in-town member, Lily Vanessa . . .

a pizza party invitation like those she sold to Morelli's Pizza Parlor for herself.

Movement behind her dimly lit windows made her look up, then stare hard through the dark glass to the terrace.

"What's wrong, Beck?" Tricia asked.

Following Becky's gaze, Tricia turned to the window and shrieked, "What's out there? What is that? What . . . is . . . it. . . ?"

Suddenly, all of them gaped at the strange dark shape and screamed wildly.

"It's a monster!" Cara yelled. "A huge monster! And it's coming for us!"

Tricia asked, "Are the French doors locked?"

Becky replied shakily, "I always lock them. Let's hope I didn't forget today!"

Jess hissed, "Why doesn't Lass bark out there?"

Becky whispered, "Mr. B takes him downstairs at night."

Still shaking, she made herself stand up.

Whatever was out there was huge, all right. Nearly the size of a pony, but with short legs, close to the ground. And now it crept and thumped along on the terrace.

All at once, she knew what it was.

"It's Quinn!" she whispered. "It's Quinn dressed up like a giant armadillo. That's why he made such a big deal about what real ones look like. That has to be it. Let's pretend to be scared and race to the bathroom, like we're going to lock ourselves in."

Shrieking loudly, they all ran to the bathroom, and Becky turned off her bedroom light on the way. Once in the bathroom, they grabbed the water balloons from the bathtub.

"Everyone ready?" she asked.

"Ready!" they answered.

"I'll open the doors," she whispered. "Just be sure none of the balloons break in my room."

"We're ready!"

Becky turned off the bathroom light, too, then opened the door. They crept into her darkened bedroom and toward the terrace doors, Becky leading the way.

The "monster" roamed back and forth between the white terrace railing and her French doors, thumping along more and more loudly.

Becky stopped at the French doors.

Behind her, Cara whispered, "What if it's not Quinn?"

"It has to be," Becky whispered back. "If it's not, whoever or whatever it is, is going to get drenched."

Reaching up, she flipped the lock, whipped the doors open, and flung one water balloon after another at the dark shape. As the balloons burst on it, she shouted, "Got you, you stupid armadillo! Got you again!"

Jumping aside, she yelled, "Let him have it!"

The other TCCers shouted and bombarded the armadillo monster with water balloons, making it back away fast.

Becky flipped on the outside terrace light. "Well, well, if it isn't an armadillo wearing a brown garbage bag! And with lizard skin and bands painted on it. Just look at that artwork! Good try, Quinn, but not good enough. We knew you'd try something!"

The outside lights went on down by the garage, illuminating the driveway and the side yard. From the lower terrace, Mr. B yelled, "Anything wrong up there, girls?"

"Attack of the giant armadillo monster," Becky called down to him. "But it's nothing the TCCers can't handle."

The armadillo monster stood up, and its sandaled feet and blue-jeaned legs looked exactly like Quinn's. His long arms reached through holes in the brown plastic bag, and while they all laughed, he swung himself over the terrace railing into a pepper tree.

"Go, armadillo monster, go!" they yelled. "Go, armadillo, go!"

As he disappeared into the leafy darkness on the unlit side of the house, the TCCers laughed wildly.

Jess gasped, "First garbage bag I've ever seen with skinny arms and legs!"

"What next?" Becky asked, then bent over laughing. Catching her breath, she choked out, "What will Quinn think of next?" What a relief it was to laugh. Of course,

45

Quinn wouldn't like it if he knew he'd actually helped her to lighten up. But right now, a little comic relief felt good.

Tricia held her sides. "You just have to stay one step ahead of him, Beck," she gasped. "Just one step!"

"Maybe you should hypnotize him!" Cara suggested, making them laugh all the harder.

Melanie managed to get out, "You can't let him get the better of you!"

"Exactly the problem!" Becky said. She tried to be serious for an instant, before another bubble of laughter escaped her. "What if I want to take a bath? I don't think I can keep my bathtub filled with water balloons forever!"

"Why not take a bath with them?" Tricia joked.

"Why not?" Becky answered, imagining the balloons bursting beneath her. "Why not?"

Then a thought struck her, making her heart hurt. She stopped laughing, but her friends didn't seem to notice. Would she ever have times like this with them again after tonight . . . now that she was no longer president?

CHAPTER

4

The next morning on the way to church, Becky, Cara, and Jess rode in the backseat of Mom's green Oldsmobile, Becky in the middle. Amanda sat in front with Mom.

Melanie, Tricia, and Quinn rode with Mr. B in his dark blue Cadillac, following them. His older sons, Jonathan and Charlie, had left earlier to pick up friends.

As Mom drove along on the palm tree-lined road toward church, Cara asked, "Would it be too much trouble, Mrs. Bradshaw, to take me home now? I . . . I don't feel well."

"What's wrong, Cara?" Becky asked with concern.

Cara lifted her shoulders in an uneasy shrug. "My stomach . . . feels weird. I'll have to come back to your house for my bike tomorrow. Or maybe Dad can pick up the bike with our van."

"Of course, we'll drop you off at your house first, Cara," Mom said. She handed the car phone over the front seat to

Becky. "Beck, why don't you dial up Paul so he doesn't wonder why we're turning in a new direction."

Becky found his car phone number taped to Mom's phone and dialed. Probably Mr. B was telling Melanie, Tricia, and Quinn some knock-knock jokes now. She punched in the phone number and listened for it to ring.

"Here, it's ringing," she said, quickly handing the phone to her mother.

"Hi, dear," Mom said. "We just wanted to let you know we're taking Cara home first. She doesn't feel well." Mom listened for a moment. "Okay. Save me a seat at church, and tell the girls to save seats for Jess and Becky at the youth group meeting. Love you."

Gr-r-r! Becky thought. Did Mom have to say "love you" so everyone could hear?

Becky glanced sideways at Jess, who grinned at her with understanding. *Embarrassing!* At least her friends knew a lot about older brothers and parents. Besides, it was better than if her mother had let out a loud "Hate you!" at Mr. B.

"Sorry to be so much trouble," Cara apologized.

"It's no trouble," Becky assured her. "You'd bring me home if I felt sick, wouldn't you?"

"Right," Cara answered, looking a little guilty.

"I know you would," Becky replied. "That reminds me of Jesus saying 'Do unto others as you would have them do unto you.' The Golden Rule."

Cara nodded again.

Strange, but Cara didn't look sick. In fact, she looked very healthy and actually beautiful in her flowery yellow-and-white summer dress. Maybe she just didn't want to go to the youth group meeting. No, that didn't make sense.

She'd been attending youth meetings and parties since early summer.

"I hope you don't miss the youth group party tonight, too," Becky told her. "Maybe you'll feel better."

Cara shrugged again. "I'll see how I feel."

"Feel well," Jess ordered. "Feel well."

"I'll try," Cara answered with a half smile.

"Just think about the great armadillo monster scare last night," Jess told her.

Cara gave them another weak half smile.

Mom and Amanda knew that Quinn had tried to scare them, but they didn't know all about what he'd done. And funny or not, Mr. B was going to have a talk with Quinn about "intruding" into the slumber party.

Jess told Becky, "Don't forget to see if we can borrow Quinn's armadillo outfit for Morning Fun for Kids."

"Let's hope he's willing," Becky answered. "He's always so . . . difficult."

She glanced toward the front seat. Thank goodness, Mom and Amanda were busy talking and hadn't heard her.

Ten minutes later, they drove into their old neighborhood.

"Hey, there's our old house!" Amanda piped from her seat.

"Never mind," Becky answered. She looked away quickly, but the image of her old house was already in her brain. Their old house might be the smallest model in Santa Rosita Estates, but it was charming with its Spanish-style arches and red-tiled roof. She'd always loved it. It felt like a home should.

Down the street, they dropped Cara off at her equally

small house. "Thanks, I had a great time," Cara told Becky. "Thank you for driving me home, Mrs. Bradshaw."

"Is someone here to let you in?" Mom asked her.

"If not, I know where the key is hidden," Cara replied. "Don't worry. It's fine. In fact, here comes Dad's van now."

Everyone in the car called out get-wells to Cara, and at the last moment, Becky added, "We'll pray for you to get better fast!"

Cara's half smile faded, but she nodded, slammed the car door, and turned to trudge up her driveway.

"Did you see Cara's face? Do you think she *doesn't* want us to pray for her?" Becky asked Jess.

Jess said a most definite, "It confused me, too. I can't believe she'd feel that way."

———

When they arrived at Santa Rosita Community Church, the front and side parking lots were already filled. Mom pulled up by the curb. "I'll drop you girls off in front if you'll take Amanda to her Sunday school class."

"Deal," Becky answered.

They climbed out of the car, and Becky noticed the church sidewalks were almost deserted. It was an unusual sight for their busy church on Sunday mornings. Probably everyone was in the sanctuary or their classrooms by now.

As they neared the sanctuary, a spindly, gray-haired woman rounded the corner. Miss Ida Burston waved a gangly arm at them excitedly, then rushed over.

"I'm so glad to see you girls," she declared breathlessly. "You made such a difference in my life, especially your friend Lily Vanessa when she sang in church last Sunday.

God sure touched my soul. I don't know how I can ever thank you for getting me to come to this church!"

Becky didn't know what to say.

Amanda blurted, "Are you Cat Woman, the one with the goat, Brutus . . . and hundreds of cats?"

"Amanda! That's rude," Becky warned.

Miss Ida laughed. "It's all right. I know people have called me Cat Woman for years. You know what? I didn't like it, but even that's fine with me now. I've been reading my old Bible every spare minute, and I've never in my life had such joy! Pure joy!"

"All right!" Jess answered. "I wish you could have gone to Israel with some of the people from this church. Lots of us were baptized in the Jordan River."

Miss Ida closed her eyes, smiled, and lifted her long, wrinkled neck skyward. "Oh, how I do wish I could have gone, too. 'Course, I wouldn't have been able to afford it. But you know what? I'm having joy right here . . . joy no matter where I am . . . joy bubbling up from deep in my soul."

Becky couldn't help beaming. "I'm glad to hear it, Miss Ida. I'll call Lily Vanessa and tell her. She'll be glad to hear it!"

"Just tell her I'm walkin' on air," Miss Ida replied. "Purely walkin' on air." She glanced at her watch. "Good grief, I'm late . . . and you must be late for your youth class, too. See you."

She started off quickly, then turned and called out, "God bless you girls."

"Thank you," Becky returned.

"Thanks a lot," Jess answered as they started off again toward the classrooms.

"She's nice," Amanda decided aloud. "She's very nice, even if everyone did call her Cat Woman."

Becky nodded. "Come on, Amanda, let's hurry."

"Working for Miss Ida was a worthwhile job," Jess remarked.

"I guess so!" Becky agreed. Actually, it had been a fierce job, taking care of Miss Ida's animals. And there'd been the fire on her property, too. God sure must have wanted the TCCers to be working there right then.

Finally, they neared Amanda's classroom.

"I can go alone now," Amanda insisted. "You don't have to stick your heads in the room, either."

Amanda opened the door herself, and Becky saw Miss Gardner directing the little kids singing. They wagged their pointer fingers like candles and sang, "This Little Light of Mine," just as they had for Youth Sunday last week.

Beaming as she closed the door, Amanda whispered to Becky and Jess, "I know that song!"

Becky just smiled.

"Whew!" she said to Jess as they started off toward their youth room. "I sure wouldn't want to teach all of those little kids. I think I'd go crazy."

Jess laughed. "That's probably what some people say about teaching our class. I'll bet they do."

"Quinn's going to be in the first part of our class today," Becky said. "Mr. B gave him a choice of going to church with Mom and him or going to the youth group class. He didn't want to go to either."

"I'll bet he didn't," Jess said. "Sounds like a brother."

At least they'd only have to put up with Quinn during the opening part of class. After the praise songs, he'd leave with the other high school kids to go to their rooms. Late as it was when they arrived in their classroom, the high school kids hadn't left yet.

"Come in, ladies," Bear said with a big smile. Their youth minister—called Ted Iddings by the adults—wasn't being a grouchy bear at all about their being so late. In fact, his Hawaiian shirt made him look like a friendly teddy bear.

He held his guitar, waiting to play. "Have a seat. We're doing things differently today, but first we'll have our last praise song, 'Our God is an Awesome God.' "

Becky grabbed a song sheet from the table near the door and led the way in. In the middle of the room, Tricia and Melanie waved them over to two empty seats by them. *All right*, Becky thought, even though they had to climb over kids' legs to get there. The only bad thing was having to pass by Quinn. He sat in an aisle chair, his long legs blocking the way.

Becky whispered, "Excuse me, Quinn."

He barely pulled his legs back.

"Excuse me, please, Quinn!" she whispered again.

Nearby, kids watched, and finally he pulled his legs in.

Everyone sang now, and Becky and Jess sang with them as they struggled onward to their seats. After having to crawl over Quinn, it was a relief to sing about serving "an awesome God" instead of feeling grouchy about Quinn. *People can be awful*, Becky thought, *but God is always awesome*.

As she sang along about Him reigning in heaven above, it struck her that she hadn't been very godly to Quinn. She hadn't been forgiving or loving. He sat five or six people away, and when she glanced at him, he was watching her.

Help me, Jesus, she prayed with her eyes open, then managed to give Quinn a small smile. If only Quinn could have joy like Miss Ida! If only—

He glared and turned away.

Help me, Jesus! she prayed again and tried to focus on worshipping God. It was a shame they'd missed most of the praise songs because she really liked to sing them.

Bear settled his guitar on a nearby table. "Hey, gang, that was a great Youth Sunday last week. I'm really proud of you. Lots of people have said good things about it."

He glanced at the TCCers. "Your friend Lily Vanessa was wonderful on 'Amazing Grace.' Please thank her again for us. In my mind's eye, I can still see everyone in the congregation holding hands and praising God while she sang."

Becky blurted, "I'll tell her when I call this afternoon."

"Good," Bear replied. "Glad to hear it." He turned his attention back to everyone. "Our Youth Sunday service made a difference in at least one person's eternal destiny . . . which means that you played an important role in bringing Ida Burston back to God. He has work planned for each of us, and we are in that sense responsible for others' souls. It's true that every person has to either accept or deny Jesus as their Savior for themselves. But what if we don't tell them?"

He hesitated, then asked, "How many of you here are always ready to tell a friend or a stranger about Jesus if a chance to do it comes up? How many of you?"

Only a few kids' hands were raised, including Tricia's. Becky considered Bear's question. If a chance came up to tell about Jesus, she'd do it *if* she could. *If* was the question.

She inched her hand upward. Beside her, Jess raised her hand slowly, too. Melanie barely raised her hand at all.

Becky darted a glance at Quinn. He'd sprawled out even more, and his eyes were shut as if he were asleep. Probably he hated being there.

Bear shook his head. "Only a few hands went right up. The rest of you were slower on the draw, probably because you're a little uncertain."

Uncertain is the word for it, Becky thought.

"Telling people about Jesus is something each of us should be ready to do at any moment. Jesus says in scripture, 'I am the way and the truth and the life. No one comes to the Father except through me.' "

Bear paused. "What kind of a Christian are you if you're not willing to tell others about Jesus?"

"Not a very loving one," Tricia answered. "Maybe not even a Christian at all."

Bear nodded. "Usually I send you high schoolers to your room, but today I'm keeping everyone together because your teacher's on vacation. And because this is so important. You'll all be back in school soon, and there are going to be opportunities for God to use you. We have lots of unhappy kids in our schools who could be turned around if you'd just tell them about God when He gives you a chance. How do you recognize an opportunity?"

A high school boy answered, "When someone asks you about God or church . . . or tells you about his troubles. . . ."

"Sometimes even when they don't ask or tell you," Tricia added. "Sometimes you can tell by looking when a person is unhappy. If you listen to God, you'll know if you're to tell them about Jesus . . . or maybe just invite them to church or to a youth party or to a Christian club."

Jess said, "It could be a member of your own family."

"Right," Bear said. "Very good. Now let's see exactly how to tell someone the way to God. We're going to look over this little booklet." He turned to a box on the table and took out four piles of yellowy-orange booklets. "Now, guys, if you'll help me pass these out. I'm sure they're familiar to some of you."

Everyone passed out the booklets, and Becky read, *Have You Heard of the FOUR SPIRITUAL LAWS?*

Over two years ago, when she was a new Christian, she'd read a booklet like it at Tricia's. It had really helped her to understand about Jesus.

From the corner of her eyes, she noticed Quinn pass the booklets to the person behind him.

After a while Bear said, "Let's read this together. First, it says that God loves you and has a wonderful plan for your life."

Bear called on Jess, Tricia, and others to read through the booklet. Halfway through it, he asked, "Quinn Bradshaw, what do you see on the next page?"

Quinn blinked groggily and sat up. "I . . . ah . . . didn't get one of those booklets."

Lie! Becky thought. *He must have passed all of them on and not kept one for himself on purpose.*

Suddenly, a terrible thought struck.

What if God meant for her to lead Quinn to Him?

Quinn had once said that he believed in God, but Becky knew very well that just believing in God didn't make anyone a Christian. Plenty of people believed in God and weren't actually Christians.

"Here," Bear said, "pass this booklet to Quinn."

After the class had read through it, Becky thought about how to explain salvation to others. *God loves you and offers a wonderful plan for your life. But since people are separated from God, they can't know God's love or plan unless they receive Jesus as their Savior.*

"Let's all bow our heads," Bear said.

He waited, "Now, with all heads bowed, is there anyone here who wants to accept Jesus Christ as his or her Savior? If so, quietly raise your hand."

The room grew so silent, it seemed that everyone must be holding their breath.

"There's one," Bear said. "Thank you, Lord."

Please, God, let it be Quinn! Becky silently hoped.

No one else must have raised a hand because Bear went on praying, "Lord, fill our new believer with your wonderful love and joy. Amen!"

When Becky opened her eyes, Bear beamed. "See how simple it is to lead someone to the Lord?" he asked.

She guessed if God sent someone her way to tell about Jesus, she could do it. Just so it wasn't Quinn Bradshaw!

Bear said, "If every day we'd just say, 'Here I am, Lord, use me,' our lives would be great adventures. We'd see miracles happening all around us."

Becky felt timid about it, but she silently prayed, *Here I am, Lord, use me*.

Opening her eyes again, she wondered what her "great adventure" could be.

CHAPTER

5

After a fun lunch out on the main terrace, Tricia, Jess, and Melanie went down to the garage for their bikes, thanking Becky for a great slumber party and the ride to church.

They'd no sooner ridden away than Cara's father drove up in his Flick's Videos van to get Cara's bike.

Becky walked the bike out to him. "How's Cara?"

"I think she's just tired," Mr. Hernandez answered, looking pleased at Becky's concern. "She went straight to bed. She'll be all right. She had a good time last night."

"I'm glad to hear it," Becky answered. "We missed her at church and for lunch here."

"Ah . . . I'm supposed to tell you she won't be coming to the youth group party tonight."

Becky hesitated, then said, "We'll miss her."

Even after Mr. Hernandez left, she felt unsettled about Cara missing the youth group this morning and now the party tonight. Was Cara backing away from church activities?

In the kitchen, Mom and Mr. B were beginning to prepare dinner. Mom chopped onions for the potato salad, and Mr. B was getting three chickens ready to barbecue. One thing he was insistent about was that everyone was home for Sunday night dinners. No excuses. Gram was coming for dinner, too.

As Becky passed through the kitchen, she asked him, "Would it be all right if I call Lily Vanessa in Los Angeles? You know, our when-in-town member."

"Of course," Mr. B replied. "Feel free to make a few long-distance phone calls every month, Becky."

"But let's not take advantage of the privilege," Mom put in. "It was generous enough of Paul to give you a private phone line."

Mr. B smiled. "I can't imagine Becky taking advantage."

"Thanks," Becky answered, heading out of the kitchen. "Thanks a lot!"

"Be sure to dial 'one' before Lily Vanessa's area code," Mom called after her.

"I will."

On her way upstairs, she had time to think. Despite her troubles with living here, it was true that Mr. B had been generous, but that was part of his marrying Mom, wasn't it? Maybe he wouldn't be so nice when they'd been around the house awhile longer.

In her room, she decided to call Lily Vanessa right away, before she lost her nerve. It'd be the first long-distance phone call to make herself. She thumbed through her blue address book. *Shields . . . Lily Vanessa Shields. . . .*

She found her number, remembered to dial 1, and punched in the numbers carefully.

The phone rang twice, then a musical voice answered, "This is Lily Vanessa."

"Hey!" Becky exclaimed. "It's Becky Hamilton. How are you doing?"

"Fine. I'm doing fine," Lily Vanessa answered. "In fact, I was just thinking about the TCCers and singing last Sunday in your church. I really was just thinking about it!"

"That's part of why I'm calling. At the youth meeting this morning, Bear said to be sure to thank you again. And Miss Ida said she's been 'walking on air' ever since last Sunday. She's been reading her Bible and says she has joy leaping in her heart."

"Well, praise God!" Lily Vanessa said. "That's exciting."

"Everyone loved your singing."

"I enjoyed it, too, once I got going," Lily Vanessa answered. "Especially when the congregation sang the last verse with me."

No sense in telling her that Quinn didn't like having a black girl around, that he was prejudiced, Becky decided. "Anyhow, thanks again."

"You're welcome. What's doing with the TCCers this week?"

"It's our last week of playcare. You know, Morning Fun for Kids. Tomorrow afternoon we're doing a clowning birthday party. There's lots of baby-sitting, some house-cleaning, and the usual car-washing."

"Wish I could be there to help," Lily Vanessa said. "I'd even do goat-sitting."

Becky laughed. "I'll never forget your goat-sitting for Miss Ida!"

Lily Vanessa laughed with her. "How're you doing in your new family?"

"Umm . . . no comment," Becky answered. "Except that I still miss my old house and neighborhood a lot."

"Maybe it'll be easier when you've lived at your new house for a while. Maybe your feeling like you belong in the old neighborhood will fade away."

"It hasn't so far," Becky admitted.

"Bad subject," Lily Vanessa said.

"It is," Becky said, deciding to change it herself. "The other reason I'm calling is this: On the way out of this morning's youth service, Bear stopped me to say he'd told someone in L.A. about your singing. They're looking for a singer for a big youth meeting. He wants to know if it's all right to give them your phone number."

"Sure!" Lily Vanessa answered, excited. "Sure, it is!" She paused. "Ummm . . . I have a question. Are all of the TCCers believers?"

Becky thought about it. "Most of us are. There's only one that I don't know for sure."

"That's what I thought," Lily Vanessa answered. "I'd better not say any more. I'm only guessing."

Becky had only known Lily Vanessa for a week, and she searched her brain for something else to say. "I'd like more of that jambalaya you made. That was so good."

"Next time I'm there, I'll make it again," Lily Vanessa promised.

"Great!" Becky told her. "See you then."

"Thanks for calling!"

Hanging up, Becky decided that her first long-distance call had been a success. Better phone Bear right away to say it was all right to give out Lily Vanessa's phone number for singing.

Minutes later, after she'd told him, someone knocked on her bedroom door. It couldn't be Amanda, who usually barged in. "Who is it?"

"It's your gram and Mr. B with goodies for your room," Gram said.

Becky heard Mr. B say, "I'll leave the step stool and rug here. I've got to get right down to check the barbecue."

"Thanks, Paul," Gram told him.

Becky rushed to the door, opened it, and gave Gram a big hug, almost crunching a colorful bag between them.

"Are you hugging me for the goodies?" Gram teased.

Becky noticed a very large package lay on the hallway floor beside the three-step stool and a chrome shower rod. "I'd hug you even if you didn't bring them."

Gram beamed. "I know it. Guess I just wanted to hear it from you." She had changed from her church clothes to a blue-green pants outfit, the same color as her eyes. Her short brown hair was neatly curled, and her round white earrings and long white matching beads set off her tan.

"You look nice, too," Becky told her.

"Compliments will get me to open the packages," Gram laughed. "Anyhow, I'm dying to show you what I've found for your bathroom. But first, let's install the shower rod and curtain."

"I'll carry in the step stool," Becky offered. She grabbed the step stool and led the way into her bathroom.

"I can't wait to see the finished product," Gram said,

joining her. "I've seen it in my mind's eye, but reality can be different."

"How can you see it in your mind's eye?" Becky asked.

"Hmm . . . never thought much about it. I just pictured your bathroom with the new shower curtain and rug."

"I should try to do that," Becky decided. "Tell me more about decorating in case I decide to be an interior designer."

"There's a lot to it," Gram answered as they began to put up the shower rod. "For example, if an interior designer sees something exactly right for a room, she buys it then, especially when it's a bargain like these things were. But she should know if the client can afford it."

Gram laughed. "I knew you could!"

"Yeah," Becky said, sobering at a thought. The more Mr. B bought for her room and did for her in any way, the deeper in debt she'd be to him, though.

She decided not to mention it to Gram. Instead, she busied herself helping her put up the chrome shower rod and then the shower curtain.

"I thought the puffy valance on top would go well with your white balloon window shade," Gram added. "The question is, does my client—that's you, Beck—like it?"

Becky stood back to study the effect. "I thought we didn't want any more white in the room, but the shower curtain is perfect with the window shade."

"Glad you like it," Gram said. "I didn't think we'd want a shower curtain to stand out too much." Still on the short stepladder, she puffed out the valance fabric here and there. "The silkiness also softens the feeling of hardness from so much tile in the room, too."

"It does. How did you know it would?"

Gram rolled her eyes. "Experience. I've been in the decorating business for a long, long time. Besides, I know what you like. You like things cheerful and beautiful because that's how you are."

Becky smiled. "You're the best grandmother in the world."

"Glad you think so," Gram answered, climbing down the step stool. "Especially since I'm the only grandmother you have who lives close by. Have you written to your Hamilton grandparents in Indiana lately?"

"Only a card after we moved into this house," Becky answered. "I'll write tomorrow. Guess I'd better do it before school starts."

"They must miss you," Gram said and gave Becky a hug. "I'd feel terrible if I didn't live near you."

"So would I," Becky admitted, hugging her back. "I'll write them tomorrow or maybe call them."

Gram carried the step stool out into the bedroom, then they opened the huge package.

A big, fluffy yellow rug!

They spread it across the white tile bathroom floor.

"Perfect," Becky pronounced as they stood back. "It cheers up the whole room and looks great with the sunflowers. Somehow it softens the room, too."

"Exactly what I'd hoped," Gram said.

After a moment, Gram asked, "Do you feel more at home here yet?"

Becky shrugged and led the way out into her bedroom. "It's a nice house, but I'm still not used to it."

"How about Amanda?"

"She has a new friend, Samantha, down the street.

They're playing now. She misses Bryan Bennett, though."

Gram nodded. "I'm not surprised." She laughed. "Especially since they say they're going to get married someday."

Becky had to smile herself, since Bryan was only five years old like Amanda.

"How are things going with Quinn?" Gram asked.

Becky felt her smile fading. "Not so good. Sometimes I think he's jealous of Amanda and me—"

"Maybe so. It might be he's also jealous of his older brothers."

"Why would he be jealous of them?" Becky inquired.

Gram raised her eyebrows. "They're more easygoing. Quinn seems to have a more difficult time dealing with life."

Becky gave it some thought. "He doesn't mind Mom being in his family as much as he does Amanda and me. But Mom makes his favorite cookies and cakes. Tonight she's making his favorite potato salad. It's hot potato salad with bacon."

"No wonder! Who wouldn't like someone doing that?"

I don't like it! Becky thought.

Gram eyed her carefully. "Are you maybe a little jealous of your mom's attention to Quinn? And to Jonathan and Charlie. . . ?"

"Ummm . . . maybe a little. How'd you know?"

Gram sighed. "Because it's only human nature to be un-easy in a newly blended family. The trouble with getting older is that sometimes you understand more about people than you want to know."

Becky smiled at her grandmother. "I'm glad you under-stand me."

"Me too," Gram said with a smile.

On the way downstairs, Amanda burst through the front door. "Hi, Gram! You know what the kids around here say?"

"What do they say?" Gram inquired.

"Yeah, what do they say?" Becky asked, since she'd yet to meet anyone her age in the neighborhood.

Amanda chanted, "Liar, liar, pants on fire, nose as long as a telephone wire!"

Becky bit back a smile, and Gram gave a laugh. "That's just teasing, Amanda. But it is teasing about lying, and we wouldn't want to be known as liars. Anything else the kids around here say?"

Amanda nodded grimly. "Cinderella, dressed in yella, went upstairs to kiss a fella. Made a mistake and kissed a snake. How many doctors did it take?"

"Sounds like jump-rope talk to me," Gram remarked.

"That's what it is," Amanda admitted. "That's what Samantha Edwards told me."

Amanda was so serious that Becky almost laughed out loud.

"I remember one myself," Gram said. "Let's see now. Ah yes, 'Not last night, but the night before . . . twenty-four robbers came knocking at my door. As I ran out, they ran in, hit me on the head with a rolling pin. . . . ' "

"That's it?" Becky asked.

Gram laughed. "That's all I remember."

Sometimes Gram can be so funny, Becky thought. *And sometimes Amanda is, too.*

———

A pleasant ocean breeze cooled the terrace as Becky and Gram pulled the big wooden table into the shade. Jonathan and Charlie coaxed Bullwinkle into his doggie yard, and Lass looked down longingly from the upstairs terrace. Seeing her watch him, he gave a mournful, "Woof!"

"You've been fed!" she called up to him. "I'll be up there in a while, don't worry!"

She began to set the table for dinner, and nearby, Mr. B finished cooking the chicken pieces on the barbecue. So far, everything was fine, but then Quinn wasn't here yet.

Before long, he arrived to help his brothers carry out the green beans, stuffed tomatoes, and potato salad. Jonathan and Charlie acted cheerful about helping, but Quinn looked grim. Becky compared him with his older brothers. Yep, Gram was right; they were a lot more relaxed than Quinn.

Finally, everyone sat down and Mr. B said grace.

When he'd finished and began to pass around the platter of chicken pieces, Becky decided that this was her chance. Quinn was seated straight across the table, and she asked him, "May the Twelve Candles Club borrow your armadillo outfit for our playcare tomorrow morning?"

Quinn was grabbing for the bowl of potato salad, and he glared over the bowl at her.

Mr. B glanced at Quinn with pretended innocence. "What armadillo outfit would that be?"

"Just something crazy," Quinn answered.

"May we borrow it for tomorrow morning?" Becky persisted. If he was going to be difficult, she was going to say so everyone could hear: *The armadillo outfit you wore last night when you tried to scare us at my slumber party . . . the armadillo outfit you wore when you weren't supposed to bother us at all.*

His dark eyes flashed at her through his gold wire glasses. "Sure," he replied grumpily. "It's out in the big garbage can."

"Thanks," Becky told him. "I'll get it later."

Everyone else seemed interested, but no one said a word—not even Amanda. Maybe they didn't want to start dinner off with trouble.

"How was your slumber party?" Jonathan asked. He was twenty-two years old and tall, almost blond, and so handsome that Becky always felt tempted to stare at him. He was going to college to be a lawyer.

"The slumber party was fine, thanks," Becky answered.

Charlie grinned. He was shorter than Jonathan and twenty years old. He looked like a Charlie should—friendly with light brown curly hair. "I heard you girls laughing and having a good time."

"We did," Becky agreed.

"And squealing," Quinn said grimly. "I heard lots and lots of squealing."

Passing the green beans, Gram put in, "It's not a good slumber party without squealing. Believe me, I remember."

"I do, too," Mom added. "Believe it or not!"

"Can't say I do," Mr. B joked. "Guys don't seem to have slumber parties, but I do remember some tricks on camping trips. I can't say I was always innocent, either."

"Not you, Dad!" Charlie teased.

Everyone chuckled, then got busy eating, but Quinn took time to glare at her again.

"Children!" he muttered under his breath, then he bit

into his piece of chicken angrily.

Mr. B asked Amanda about her Sunday school class, and she told what she'd learned about being friends with Jesus.

"How about your youth class, Becky?" Mom asked.

"It was about leading people to the Lord," she answered.

"Good," Mom said. "I'm glad to hear it."

Everyone quieted, and Becky thought about saying that Quinn had been in the class, too. But seeing his grouchy look, she decided to keep quiet. She looked around the table and noticed that everyone seemed to be careful of Quinn.

As she bit into a chicken leg, she couldn't imagine how things would ever be right unless someone led him to Jesus. Quinn was a problem for the entire family, not just for her.

Suddenly, she felt too tired to go to the youth group party tonight . . . just too tired to do anything.

CHAPTER

6

The next morning, Becky rode in the backseat as Mr. B and Mom drove her to Morning Fun for Kids. She glanced out the window. The Santa Rosita Estates houses they passed weren't nearly as nice as those in Mr. B's neighborhood, but her this-really-is-home feeling was not fading away.

Her chest squeezed tight.

It was no easier today to ride along on her old street, La Crescenta, than it'd been yesterday. This morning she made herself look at her old house with red geraniums and bougainvillea blooming all around it. Seeing the "For Sale" sign hurt, but at least the house wasn't sold yet.

She glanced away quickly as Mr. B drove into Tricia's driveway next door.

Mom told him, "I forgot to tell you, the realtor called this morning. It seems they have two families interested in buying the house."

Becky's spirits drooped even lower. It was bad enough to have left her old house; now she didn't know how she'd be able to endure someone else living in it . . . even living in her old room!

"Two families are interested!" Mr. B replied. "You're serious?"

"I'm serious," Mom said. "Both families need to move quickly, before school starts."

Becky sat like a stone statue in the backseat, even after Mr. B stopped the car.

"Aren't you going to get out, Beck?" Mom asked her.

"Oh!" Becky exclaimed, shaking herself a little. "Sure! Thanks for driving me here."

Still dazed, she grabbed her blue nylon overnight tote, since she was spending the night with Tricia.

"Don't forget your clown outfit," Mom said.

"Thanks." She took her blue-and-white polka-dotted clown costume from the clothes-carrying hook. She'd almost forgotten about it and the clown birthday party the TCCers had signed up for this afternoon.

"And the green bag," Mom added. "Are you all right, Becky?"

"Yeah, thanks," she answered, feeling stupid.

Finally she had everything: her overnight clothes, the clown outfit, and the bag that held the armadillo outfit and her art supplies.

"See you Tuesday," Becky told them and climbed out, her hands full. "I'll call and let you know when."

As she walked up Tricia's driveway, Becky kept her eyes on the Bennetts' garage, then on the breezeway gate. Anything to keep from seeing her old house next door. She noted the usual yellow poster taped to the Bennetts' gate.

MORNING FUN FOR KIDS
PLEASE KNOCK ON GATE

The poster was getting a little shabby, she decided. Tears welled in her eyes. No sense in making another poster now . . . not with summer and her TCC days almost over.

She blinked hard and set her overnight tote and the green garbage bag down on the sidewalk. Stretching, she reached over the high wooden gate to undo the latch, then let herself in. Instead of yelling her usual "I'm here!" she made her way quietly through the breezeway. The card table with the TCC sign-in clipboards were already in place, she noticed. She'd been at the Bennetts' house thousands of times, but this morning she looked at the yard and the colorful gym set and sandbox with sad eyes.

Finally, she stepped into the yard.

No one there.

The yard had been perfect this summer for Morning Fun for Kids, their playcare for the four- to seven-year-old Funners. The redwood picnic table and benches had worked well for arts and crafts, and the pass-through shelf from the kitchen window helped with serving snacks. Butterscotch, the Bennetts' old cat, sat like a princess overlooking the quiet scene. Even the fresh peach color of the two-story house made the setting look cheerful and welcoming for Funners.

Tricia stepped from the back door. "Hey, Beck, you're early! I didn't hear you come in."

"I didn't yell," Becky answered. "Anyhow, Mom and

Mr. B are meeting Gram to shop for faucets, so they dropped me off on the way."

"Do you have the armadillo outfit?" Tricia asked.

"It's in here," Becky said, carrying the big green garbage bag to the table.

Tricia opened the bag and peered inside. "Hmmm . . . an armadillo-decorated brown garbage bag. Who except Quinn could have thought of it?"

"No one," Becky agreed.

Tricia shrugged. "I still haven't decided how to use an armadillo costume for Magic Carpet, but I'll figure out something." She began to empty the bag. "Hey, I thought armadillos had big tails."

"Quinn's not that artistic," Becky said. Her voice trembled, but Tricia didn't seem to notice. Becky made herself go on. "I'm not sure I could attach a tail to it myself."

"What's this hobby horse on a stick doing in here?" Tricia asked, pulling it out.

"That was the armadillo's pointy head."

"A good thing Quinn waited until dark," Tricia remarked. "Actually, it's not such a bad idea, is it?"

"I guess not," Becky answered. "Anyhow, I brought a big picture of an armadillo and lots of brown and yellow crayons. They're in the yellow folder."

"Great." Tricia examined the armadillo picture, then returned it to the folder on the table. "Come on in. I'll put the armadillo costume stuff in the family room closet, so it's close by."

That done, she added, "Let's take your overnight stuff upstairs now. We can hang your clown outfit there, too, before it's claimed by the Funners."

"Sure."

Taking the clown outfit from her, Tricia scrutinized her. "Hey, what's wrong, Beck?"

"Nothing new," Becky answered. Tears burst to her eyes, and she blinked them away. "It's just that I still . . . I still have a hard time seeing . . . my old house."

"Oh, Becky . . . so do I sometimes," Tricia admitted. "It's just not the same without you living next door. I don't think I'll ever get used to it."

Becky blinked hard again. "We have to get used to it, that's all. When I phoned Lily Vanessa yesterday, she said after a while I'd get used to not living here . . . and that the hurt would fade away. It hasn't so far, though. Boy, is that the truth. It sure hasn't so far."

Bryan came racing down the stairs. "Where's Amanda?"

"Not coming today," Becky told him. No sense in telling him she'd be playing with her new friend, Samantha, in the new neighborhood. It'd only make him feel bad. "I think she might come Wednesday."

"Oh," he answered sadly. "I hope so."

Another thing in their lives changing, she thought.

Tricia's seven-year-old sister, Suzanne, came out on the upstairs landing. "Isn't Amanda coming?" she asked.

"Not today," Becky told her.

"I wish she was here today!" Suzanne wailed. "I wish you'd never moved away!" She ran back into her room and slammed the door.

Once inside Tricia's bedroom, Becky said, "Ummm . . . do you suppose you could close your curtain . . . the one that faces—"

"Sure," Tricia interrupted, and Becky was glad she

hadn't had to say, *the one that faces my old house.*

She put her overnight tote at the foot of Tricia's guest bed and drew a breath of relief as Tricia quickly pulled the white drapes together. That still left the open window facing the front, which gave them plenty of light. The room was great, like a green-and-white garden overlooking the trees alongside the street.

Tricia's green-and-white polka-dotted clown outfit hung on a hook near her closet, and she hung Becky's clown outfit on a hook next to it. She turned to Becky. "How's that?"

"That's fine. Thanks."

"Everything's going to be all right," Tricia told her. "Now let's think about something else."

"Like what?"

A car door slammed outside, and they peered down to the street. "Yipes, Jojo and Jimjim Davis are early!" Tricia exclaimed. "Come on, let's get down there."

Before long, they were outside by the breezeway gate.

"Knock-knock! Knock-knock!" Jojo and Jimjim called out with a laugh.

Tricia threw open the gate, and Mrs. Davis stood laughing with her five-year-old, green-eyed, freckled identical twins.

At the sight of their wide grins, Becky had to smile herself. Jojo and Jimjim were something else.

Mrs. Davis said, "I'm sorry, I don't know how we got here so early this morning."

"That's fine," Tricia assured her.

The next moment, Jojo and Jimjim bolted in through the breezeway, yelling in their secret twin language, "Umpty-dundle-dum-umpty-umpty-dundle-dun-dun!" They raced wildly for the swings.

Jess, Cara, and Melanie rode their bikes up the driveway. "Here come the other TCCers," Becky told Mrs. Davis.

Mrs. Davis began to fill out the sign-in sheet. "I don't know what I'd have done without your playcare this summer. Jojo and Jimjim have been a handful."

You can say that again, Becky felt like saying.

Instead, she replied, "They're always . . . interesting."

Mrs. Davis gave a laugh. "That's for sure. Thank you for being so kind, Becky."

They all laughed and turned to watch Jojo and Jimjim shriek and pump higher and higher on the swings.

Mrs. Davis had no more than returned the sign-in clipboard than Jess, Cara, and Melanie opened the garage's side door and hopped down the two steps.

"Hey-hey," they called out as they hurried into the breezeway. "We're here!"

"And ready for anything!" Jess declared.

"We may have anything today," Becky told her.

Car doors began to slam out by the street, and Tricia said, "Here come the Funners! I put the list of activities on the table."

Becky made a run for the table with Jess, Cara, and Melanie. It helped to be prepared.

The list said,

1. Magic Carpet game (Tricia & Cara). Armadillo theme (Becky and Jess get arts and crafts ready).
2. Beanbag fun (Jess, Cara, & Melanie.)
3. Gymnastics (Jess) or crafts (Becky). (Cara, Tricia,

and Melanie get out midmorning snacks.)

4. Midmorning snacks (everyone helps).
5. Free time for swings, playing with boxes, etc. (all except Becky and Melanie, who stay with crafts).
6. Sand castle contest (all except Becky and Melanie, who stay with crafts).

Before long, the yard filled with kids yelling and running. Pinky Royster, who'd been homeless and didn't talk much, somersaulted around the yard. Bryan and Suzanne Bennett played "Jack in the Box," jumping up and down. Sam Miller peered around the yard mischievously. When Wanda Lester and Wendy Johnson arrived, he chased after them and yanked their ponytails.

"If only we could hypnotize these kids!" Cara said as if she really meant it.

"You and your hypnotizing!" Jess laughed.

There it is again, Cara talking about hypnotizing, Becky thought. She should have asked Bear about it. Maybe she could call him tonight.

"Fifteen Funners today!" Jess said. "Fifteen!"

"That's not as bad as forty-five, like on the cruise ship!" Melanie answered.

Becky helped Tricia carry the raggedy brown rug from the garage. Once they were on the lawn, the Funners helped roll out the rug.

When it was ready, Tricia stood on the front edge of it and announced, "Okay, Funners, we're going to f-l-y a-w-a-y on this wonderful m-a-g-i-c c-a-r-p-e-t! Everyone come sit down on our m-a-g-i-c c-a-r-p-e-t so we can get ready to f-l-y! F-l-y—f-l-y—f-l-y—f-l-y!" The big, green garbage bag lay ready by her feet.

As usual, Tricia made the Magic Carpet Ride sound so mysterious and exciting that the Funners stopped everything and hurried to sit on the old rug. She had taken them on imaginary trips into space, to a pirates' island, a Chinese New Year's parade, and lots of other places.

Cara stood on the back of the "magic carpet" and shouted, "Last call for the Magic Carpet Ride, Funners! Last call!"

Becky headed for the redwood table to get out the armadillo artwork. Seated, she began to trace armadillo outlines on papers for the Funners to color. Luckily, Jess was coming to help.

Tricia raised her hands. "Last call for F-u-n-n-e-r-s!" She wore white shorts and a white T-shirt, and the morning breeze stirred her long, reddish-blond hair, making her appear even more dramatic. She also looked determined to hold their attention, even if it killed her.

"Before we fly away, Funners, we should know each others' names!" she told them. "Now, I know we all have name tags, but not all of us can read yet. Let's call out our names and tell how o-l-d we are."

"Craig Leonard! Seven years old!" Craig shouted.

"Sam Miller! Seven!"

"Wanda Lester. Six," yelled Wanda, who wasn't as shy as when she first began to attend.

"Wendy Johnson!" her friend called out. "I'm six."

Jojo and Jimjim Davis yelled, "Umpty-um-la-da-da!"

Tricia just smiled at them.

Suzanne Bennett called out her name and "Seven!" Then Sally Lowe, Blake Berenson, and Bryan announced their names, and "Five!" Pinky Royster held up five fingers.

When everyone there had identified themselves, Tricia called out, "W-e-l-c-o-m-e, F-u-n-n-e-r-s! Now everyone grab hold to the edges of our m-a-g-i-c c-a-r-p-e-t." Once they'd all grabbed hold, she added, "Now everyone close your eyes and use your imaginations."

The Funners closed their eyes, and Tricia quickly slipped the armadillo outfit over her shorts and tee.

"All right, Funners, we're going to A-r-m-a-d-i-l-l-o L-a-n-d, where these c-r-a-f-t-y a-n-i-m-a-l-s c-r-e-e-p out at night in s-e-a-r-c-h of i-n-s-e-c-t-s and c-r-a-y-f-i-s-h. We're going to A-r-m-a-d-i-l-l-o Land!"

Finally Tricia was in the "armadillo outfit," including its hobby-horse head. "Funners, you can o-p-e-n y-o-u-r e-y-e-s n-o-w!" she called out.

The kids opened their eyes and yelled, "Yiiiiiiii!"

A horrible thought struck Becky—a thought that had nothing to do with the armadillo outfit Tricia wore.

Wasn't what Tricia called "magic" a lot like hypnotism? Becky wondered. Tricia was having them close their eyes and visualize stuff. Was her best friend—and the TCCers' strongest Christian—hypnotizing the Funners? On top of everything else, on Saturday night Tricia had been silent when Cara mentioned hypnosis.

She'd have to ask Tricia later. But how could she ask? How could she bring up the subject without sounding like a know-it-all? On top of everything at home going wrong, what if it ruined their friendship?

CHAPTER

7

After Morning Fun for Kids, Becky didn't have her bike along, so she walked while the TCCers rode their bikes to Jess's house for lunch. She could walk and run plenty fast, but she still was the last one there. If only she didn't feel so out of it.

Once in the kitchen, she stood at the counter, waiting behind the others to make peanut butter sandwiches while Jess got a pitcher of lemonade from the refrigerator. Paper plates were piled at one end of the counter, followed by sliced breads, peanut butter, jelly, chips, olives, pickles, and fresh veggies and fruits.

Becky helped herself to a paper plate and two slices of wheat bread. Moving along behind the others, she spread chunky peanut butter on her slices of bread. At least it smelled comforting.

Waiting, she had time to think.

How could she possibly ask Tricia if she used hypnosis for the Magic Carpet Ride? The Magic Carpet Ride had been a highlight of Morning Fun for Kids since its very beginning this summer—and every one of the Funners loved riding or flying off to imaginary places.

But wasn't hypnosis an occult practice like witchcraft, astrology, horoscopes, tarot cards, and other evil stuff?

The other TCCers laughed at something, and she glanced at Tricia. Her head was thrown back in laughter about Cara's peanut butter and green grapes sandwich. Sunshine streamed through a skylight, making Tricia's reddish-blond hair shimmer as she laughed.

This was her very best friend. No way was she going to ask her about hypnosis now and ruin everything, Becky decided. She'd have to ask Bear about it.

From the jar of pickle slices, she forked up four dripping slices to put on her peanut butter sandwich, just to be different. If Cara was going to use green grapes—

"Come *on*, Beck!" Tricia laughed. "Not you making peculiar sandwiches, too!"

"Ummm . . . think I'll have a hot pepper or two on the side," Becky remarked, trying for a sly grin. Then, to be even crazier, she put two hot peppers between the pickle slices on the peanut butter. "Just look at the color contrasts," she told them.

"You weirdo!" Jess exclaimed.

The next moment, Jess's hazel eyes twinkled. "Hmmm . . . think I'll put some chips on mine. Crushed chips and peanut butter. . . ."

"Who's weird now?" Melanie asked with a laugh. "Who's weird?" She promptly sliced up radishes and stuck them on her peanut butter. "Now, that is a nutritious sandwich and only a trifle weird."

Tricia announced, "I'll put carrot sticks on mine, but that's as far as I'm prepared to go!"

They all compared sandwiches and laughed again.

Thank goodness for the sandwich madness, Becky thought. *Anything to stop thinking about the hypnosis problem!*

They made last-minute grabs for chips and raw veggies, then headed out the back door for the patio near the swimming pool. "Wish we had time to swim," Tricia said as they sat down around the umbrella patio table. "It'd be nice and cool today, not to mention relaxing after Morning Fun for Kids."

"The birthday party's at two," Melanie reminded them. "Anyhow, we're in the umbrella's shade now."

Tricia said grace, and they began to eat.

Aughhh . . . the peppers burned! Becky removed a bite of hot peppers from her mouth, then the rest of them from her sandwich. No one seemed to notice. In fact, no one seemed to notice her much at all. She may as well have stayed home.

"Here's our party agenda for Valerie Whitley's birthday party," Melanie said. "I didn't make everyone a copy since it's similar to our usual clowning parties. We did add a new skit to make it different for kids who've been to our other birthday parties."

Who's "we"? Becky wondered.

She sat back and reminded herself that she was no longer president of the Twelve Candles Club. In fact, soon she'd be only a part-time member.

Melanie passed around the neatly printed birthday party

agenda, and Becky glanced at it, wishing she didn't feel so left out.

1. Face-painting as kids arrive
2. Hokey-Pokey
3. Sing "Old MacDonald Had a Farm"
4. Comedy Show (balloon skit, elastic skit, new pop skit)
5. Balloon animals
6. Birthday present circle
7. Clown gifts for kids

"What's this new pop skit?" Becky asked.

"Jess, you tell, since you're the one who found it," Melanie suggested. "I need to hear it again myself."

When did the others hear it? Becky wondered. *Maybe last week when she'd been busy settling in at Mr. B's house.*

"Let me think now," Jess said, then began. "The first clown carries in a card table and sets it down. Exhausted, she mops her brow. The second clown comes in, wipes her brow, and brings a pop can to the table. The third clown wipes her brow, exhausted, and opens the can. The fourth clown comes along and takes a drink from the can. The fifth clown—that's me—comes along and belches."

"Gross!" Becky exclaimed. "That's really gross."

Cara nodded. "Parents won't like the belching."

"But little kids will love it," Jess replied. "You just watch, boys will laugh like mad and girls will put their hands over their faces and giggle."

"I don't know if that's the kind of skit we want to do, either," Tricia said, "but we're desperate for new acts. Maybe we should call Mrs. Whitley and run the idea by her. Maybe it wouldn't bother her at all. Anyone want to volunteer to call her?"

No way would she do it, Becky thought. "Gross" was definitely not the direction she'd ever wanted to take the Twelve Candles Club.

"I'll do it," Jess offered, jumping up from the table. "Mom says we need to go to a big clowning workshop like they have in L.A. and San Diego. That's how to learn a lot of clowning acts."

Becky guessed she wouldn't be able to go to any clowning workshops, either. Because of moving, she'd be left out of everything.

After a while Jess returned, grinning. "Mrs. Whitley thought just like I did. The boys would love it, and the girls would giggle. She thinks it's the kind of skit that only clowns can get away with. And it gives parents an opportunity to tell their kids that belching is disgusting."

"Guess I was wrong," Becky admitted, still not convinced of it.

After lunch, they carried their paper plates to the kitchen and cleaned up, then hurried to Jess's room. Despite her gymnastic mats and equipment, Jess's room was a perfect place for clowns to get ready. Best of all, a huge mirror hung behind her ballet *barre*.

They began to change into their polka-dotted clown outfits, then to apply one another's clown makeup in front of the mirror. They'd become faster at it than when they'd first started the clowning birthday parties this summer . . . and it went a lot faster than at first, when Mrs. Bennett had done makeup for each of them.

Tricia remarked, "It's a shame Mom hasn't had time to make Melanie a clown outfit, too."

Hmmpphhh! Becky thought. *Then they won't need me at*

all! Just the thought of it made her more and more angry.

Filled with anger, Becky heard herself say rather calmly, "Melanie can wear my clown outfit."

"Are you sure, Beck?" Melanie asked with amazement.

Becky nodded. She'd gone this far, she wasn't going to back out now. "I'm sure. You just need to pull up the sleeves and legs by the elastic, since I'm taller. I . . . I don't feel well. I think maybe I should go home."

"What can you expect when you eat a peanut butter sandwich with pickles and hot peppers!" Tricia teased.

They all laughed, and Becky made a tiny smile edge her lips upward. She recalled Cara backing out of going to their church youth group last Sunday and knew that doing this was a lot like backing out. "I'll call Mom to get me. If she's not home yet, maybe Gram is."

She headed for Jess's desk to use the phone. Not even one of her so-called friends was trying to get her to stay and be in the clowning birthday party with them. Not one of them had said, *No way, Beck! We can't do a birthday party without you!* She almost cried as she dialed Mom and Mr. B's phone number.

As if that wasn't bad enough, Quinn answered the phone with an abrupt "Hello."

"Is Mom there, or your dad?"

"No. Just me," Quinn said.

"Where are they?"

He didn't sound any friendlier. "Out shopping with your grandmother, as usual. Where else?"

Becky's mind raced. Maybe Jonathan or Charlie could come for her. . . . She asked, "Are you there alone?"

"I'm here alone," Quinn stated flatly. Probably he was

tightening his jaw, as usual, and scowling.

It took an effort, but she forced herself to say, "Could you please come pick me up in Santa Rosita Estates?"

"Me pick you up? Are you kidding?"

"No, I'm not kidding," she told him. "I . . . I'm not feeling well." Worst of all, her not-feeling-well was becoming true.

"Where are you?" he growled, and, giving the address, she pretended not to notice how angry he sounded.

Fifteen minutes later, she looked out the front window as Quinn drove up in Jess's driveway in Mr. B's old tan camping van.

She grabbed the green garbage bag with the armadillo outfit and opened Jess's door.

"Bye, guys! Have a great birthday party!"

They all waved and called out good-byes, but none of them seemed to regret her leaving. Not a single one of them! They wore their colorful polka-dot clown outfits and raggedy wigs and, posing like wackos in front of Jess's ballet *barre* mirror, looked ready for lots of fun.

"Hey, guys," Tricia said to them excitedly, "I just remembered a new clown skit. It's about juggling beanbags and an upside-down 'How to Juggle' book."

Becky felt more left out than ever as she closed the door behind her.

In the van, Quinn gave her a disgusted look.

"I really appreciate your picking me up," she told him as she buckled her seat belt. "And the kids loved your armadillo outfit this morning. I've got it here. I've saved it in case you—"

"Don't talk," he interrupted, backing the van down the

driveway. "I want to concentrate on my driving."

Becky knew he didn't have much driving experience, but this was too much. She closed her eyes, and tears pressed behind her lids. At Mom's wedding, God had given her a great burst of love for Mr. B, Jonathan, Charlie, and Quinn. If only that wonderful love had lasted forever. Now she really felt sick—and on top of that, Quinn was making her feel like a nuisance.

When they arrived at home, Quinn parked the camping van in the garage and got out in a huff.

"Thanks, Quinn!" she called out, but he didn't answer. Instead, he just headed for his room beside the garages.

Bullwinkle barked at him, but Quinn didn't even have a friendly word for his own dog.

Becky trudged up the outside steps and found Jonathan reading a letter out on the main terrace. He'd probably just come home because the mail lay on the table beside him instead of on the kitchen counter.

He looked at her over the letter. "Quinn pick you up?"

Becky nodded. "I'm not feeling well." She felt so aggravated that the next words tumbled from her lips. "Not that Quinn cared much! He didn't even want me to talk to him on the drive home!"

Jonathan took a deep breath and lifted his shoulders. "Maybe you just need to be extra nice to him."

"Me be nice to him?!" Becky snapped. "What about me? He's not nice to me! He's *never* nice to me! And I'm the one who had to move to a different house and leave all of my friends. I'm the one who's had the hardest time of it."

"Quinn gave you his room and moved out to the potting shed—"

"He didn't have to move out there!" Becky objected. "He was the one who wanted to do it! Besides, there's another bedroom in the house!"

"Maybe he didn't make a good decision," Jonathan began. "Sometimes when we're upset we don't stop to make good decisions."

Becky clenched her fists at her sides. "You mean I should move out of my bedroom now that Gram has it all decorated for me? Is that what you mean?"

"Not at all," Jonathan said. "I shouldn't have stuck my nose into it. I just thought Quinn might be friendlier if you were extra nice to him."

"No one's extra nice to me!" Becky flung back again. "No one!"

"It seems to me that Dad has been," Jonathan told her. He hesitated, "And I'd like to be friends with you."

"You're way older than Amanda and me. Besides, you'll be leaving for college."

He nodded. "But that doesn't mean we can't be friends. We could be friends the rest of our lives. You're not going to be twelve years old forever."

"But you're ten years older!"

"I don't think ten years will make such a difference once you're grown up," Jonathan said.

Becky headed for the French door to the kitchen. "Maybe not," she answered. She didn't see how she could ever be friends with a twenty-two-year-old stepbrother.

"When you're twenty-two, I'll be thirty-two," Jonathan told her. "We'll have a lot more in common by then. We can begin to be friends now and then be friends the rest of our lives. Quinn's going through a difficult time, being a teenager, but you could eventually turn out to be friends with him, too. . . ."

"Thanks," she called back, unconvinced. "See you."

She let herself into the kitchen and closed the door behind her. Being friends with Quinn seemed impossible. As for being friends with Jonathan? *Twenty-two years old, thirty-two years old . . . it sounded ancient.*

At least he'd tried to be friendly, she told herself, but it didn't help much. Nothing helped much lately.

She made her way up the stairs toward her room. With Amanda and Mom and Mr. B gone, the house felt stranger than ever . . . too quiet and empty.

Upstairs, out on the terrace, Lass stood looking into a window of her French doors. He woofed and wagged his tail, glad to see her, but it still didn't cheer her. She might have a beautiful room in a very nice house now, but her family having lots more money sure wasn't making her happy.

She glanced at her alarm clock.

Almost two o'clock.

That meant the TCCers would soon be welcoming birthday party guests at Valerie Whitley's house. In just minutes, they'd begin the face painting, and the little kids would be jumping up and down with excitement. She hoped they'd do the new juggling act that Tricia had begun to tell them about—and not the gross skit. There'd be cake and ice cream and lots of fun.

Tears pressed against her eyelids again.

Everything was turning out just as she'd feared. Once she'd moved to this part of town, things weren't the same.

The other TCCers' lives were going on without her, and she'd almost never see them. Her whole life was ruined!

Jonathan had mentioned making bad decisions. If only she hadn't backed out of doing the party. If only she hadn't . . . what was it she'd done?

Suddenly, she knew.

If only she hadn't given in to feeling sorry for herself . . . and to this bad attitude!

CHAPTER

8

*B*ecky lay in her bed, staring up at the white ceiling. She guessed she should read her Bible or at least count her blessings, but she didn't feel like doing either. Now that she thought about it, she didn't feel like doing anything positive.

"Help me, Jesus," she prayed. "I don't want to be in the darkness like this."

She closed her eyes. Maybe if she slept she'd feel better. Maybe she was really getting sick.

Everything grew dark as she dozed off. Out of the darkness, skeleton fingers reached out for her. She wanted to scream, but the sound stuck in the back of her throat.

Scream! she told herself. *Scream!!!*

But not even a small *eek* squeaked out.

Shadowy figures floated through the darkness, and she twisted wildly away from them, only screaming silently in her throat. She tugged and turned away, but it didn't stop them. Finally, she turned over in bed. A nightmare . . . this was only a nightmare.

Still groggy, she closed her eyes. Before long, the dusky figures reached for her again, and she tried to tear herself away, but her body couldn't move, either.

Help! she wanted to scream, but it didn't come out. *Help me, someone, help!*

The phone rang, but it sounded far, far away. On the third ring, she hoped someone would answer it, then realized it was her private line . . . and ringing right next to her on her new white wicker nightstand. She sat up in bed groggily and picked up the receiver, fumbling and almost dropping it.

"Hello," she croaked.

"Hello . . . Becky. . . ?" A man's voice sounded familiar but far away, as if it were coming from the other side of the planet. "Is this Becky Hamilton?"

She cleared her throat. "Yes . . . yes, it is."

"It's Bear," he told her. "Did I wake you up?"

"I . . . yep, you did," she admitted. She blinked her eyes, and it seemed to clear her brain a little. "I'm glad you called, though. I was having a nightmare."

"You sound different," he said. "Are you sick?"

"I don't know. . . ."

"I called for Lily Vanessa's phone number in L.A. I know you gave it to me, but I can't seem to find it."

Becky saw her blue phone book on the nightstand's shelf. "It's in my phone book. Just a second." She thumbed through to the S's for Shields. "Here it is. Lily Vanessa Shields."

After she'd given him the number, Bear said, "We

missed you and Cara at the youth party last night. Is every-thing all right?"

"Ummm . . . I guess so."

"You don't sound very sure of it," he remarked. "Your name came to mind just a minute ago, and I knew I was supposed to call you. Are you having a hard time settling in with your new family?"

He sounded as if he truly cared and wasn't just being nosey, but she didn't want to talk about it right now.

Bear added, "I took one look at Quinn's grim face at the youth group yesterday morning, and I figured he wasn't too happy . . . and that he wasn't making your life too happy, either. Is that what it is?"

"Some of it," she told him. She could imagine Bear's concerned face.

"I'd like to be friends with Quinn," Bear said.

"I wish you could be friends with him, too."

After a long silence, he added, "Probably some of your problem is having to leave your friends in Santa Rosita Estates. Getting into a blended family and moving to a new neighborhood usually isn't the happiest situation on earth for starters."

"I guess not."

She thought, *It sure isn't here.*

"You want to pray about it before I hang up?"

Becky swallowed hard. "Yes."

"I've been concerned about Cara, too," Bear said. "She wasn't at yesterday's youth meeting or the party, either, and I notice she's been sort of backing away from us. Can you give me any hints?"

"Her family isn't religious," Becky said.

"You mean they're not Christians?" he asked.

She nodded, even though he couldn't see her. "That's what I mean, I guess. She told me her mother didn't want her to get too involved with religion."

"Guess they don't know that following Jesus is a relationship, not a religion. You know it, don't you?"

"Sometimes I forget."

"Seems everyone does," Bear said. "Me too, and I sure shouldn't, but I'm human just like everyone else."

It was surprising that he forgot, too, Becky thought.

Suddenly, she remembered something. "Is hypnotism bad . . . you know, from the occult?"

"You'd better believe it!" Bear answered. "Why? Is someone into it?"

"Maybe," she answered, thinking about Tricia and the Magic Carpet Ride. Even the word *magic* was in it. Lots of people thought some kinds of magic came from the occult.

"You're not sure?" he asked.

"No," Becky answered.

Thinking about Cara and Paige, she quickly added, "And maybe someone in someone's family, too. I . . . I'd better not say anything more about it."

"I understand," Bear replied. "Make sure they know it's bad stuff, if you can. Hypnotism, witchcraft, astrology, horoscopes, black magic, tarot cards, Ouija boards, and all the other occult practices lead into darkness . . . farther and farther away from God."

He added, "They might start out innocently, as if there's nothing bad about it. Someone says, 'Oh, let's just try it. It can't hurt us.' Sometimes they start with board games or funny little stories about witches, but eventually they can lead to horrible situations. And each of these practices seem to lead to another. They're deadly. Absolutely deadly."

"That's what I thought," Becky said.

And the Magic Carpet Ride had begun as fun . . . innocently.

"Stay away from anything occult," he added. "You know, when a person comes to know Jesus, he's transformed from dark to light. There's power in the occult, but it eventually leads to evil. You want to talk more about it?"

If only she could tell him. But it was Tricia's and Cara's business—not hers to tell. "Thanks, but I can't."

"I see," Bear said. "I do want to tell you this. Hypnosis gives another spirit control of your body, and you only want the Holy Spirit to control you, not evil spirits! If someone wants to try hypnosis on you or anyone else, run! Don't look or even listen. Just get away from them."

Becky swallowed. *Does that mean the Magic Carpet Ride?*

Bear hesitated. "You're sure you don't want to tell me?"

"I'm sure," she answered. "Positive."

He hesitated. "I respect that, Becky. Well, then, to change the subject, did you understand what I tried to explain Sunday morning about leading friends to Jesus?"

"Yes."

"Just checking," he told her. "I like to make sure I'm coming across clearly."

"You did," she assured him.

"Let's give it all to the Lord," Bear suggested. "May I pray with you now?"

"Sure," Becky answered.

She closed her eyes. It seemed strange to have the youth pastor pray with her on the phone, but Tricia had done it and so had Mom with Mrs. Bennett. Maybe lots of people prayed over telephones.

"Holy Father," Bear began, "we come to you with praise and thanksgiving for so many blessings, and especially for the blessing of your sending Jesus to be our Lord and Savior. We are just human beings, every one of us, but we know that you can change our hearts and our lives. We pray now for your joy to overflow in Becky's life . . . and for you to draw Cara and Quinn closer to you, for their salvation. . . . We pray that you would keep them from all evil and keep all evil from them. . . ."

Please, Lord, Becky prayed. *Please keep it from Cara and Tricia!*

Before long, she heard Bear say, "Amen," and she added an "Amen" herself.

After he hung up, she noticed her clock. Almost five o'clock already. The TCCers would be home from the birthday party by now, and despite everything, she was eager to hear how the party went.

Her first thought was to phone Tricia. Maybe they could discuss the Magic Carpet Ride, maybe even change its name to Story Carpet Ride.

Her second thought was to call Cara to ask how the birthday party went. Cara didn't have a really best friend among them. She didn't even have a dog like Lass to smile in the window at her like Lass was doing now. On the other hand, Cara did have Angora, her white cat.

Becky dialed the number and waited while the phone rang on the other end.

"Hello?" Cara answered.

"It's me, Becky," she told her.

"Are you all right?" Cara asked.

Becky nodded. "I slept all afternoon. I'm still groggy, but I think I'm better."

"Good," Cara said. "I was worried that maybe you'd caught whatever was wrong with me Sunday morning. Anyhow, I'm glad you're better. We missed you at the birthday party."

"I was going to ask you how the party went," Becky told her.

Cara's voice filled with surprise. "You're calling me?"

"Sure, why not?" Becky asked.

"Guess I just thought you'd call Tricia to find out—"

"No, I wanted to call *you*," Becky assured her.

Cara sounded pleased. "Thanks! It was great . . . a great party. You'll be glad to hear we didn't use the gross skit about belching. Tricia came up with a new juggling skit. Were you there when she told about it?"

"I just heard a little of it before I left," Becky answered. "It sounded good."

"It was!" Cara continued, "The kids loved the skit and everything else. It was a good party."

"Great," Becky told her. "Actually, I called for another reason, too. You know, you were talking about Paige being into . . . hypnosis. . . ."

"Yeah?"

"Well, I just wanted to warn you, Bear says it's dangerous . . . to get away and not look or even listen if someone's trying to hypnotize people."

Cara didn't answer.

Becky hurried on. "It's hard for me to talk to you about something that's probably none of my business, but I really like you, Cara. I thought you might get mad, but I don't want you to get hurt. . . ."

Cara spoke stiffly. "Let's not talk about it. Is *that* why you called?"

"Some of the reason . . . maybe half and half," Becky replied. "Half is that I wanted to hear about the birthday party, and the other half is that I wanted to warn you about hypnosis. I'm supposed to be your friend. . . ."

Cara didn't answer, but just then Paige's voice blasted out nearby, "When are you getting off that phone, Caro-leena Hernandez?"

"Umm . . . I have to run now," Cara told Becky. "Paige wants to use the phone. See you!"

"Yeah. See you."

Hanging up slowly, Becky wondered if she should have phoned at all.

————

At six-thirty, Becky's new family gathered outside to eat dinner. A warm breeze ruffled the paper napkins slightly, but otherwise it was a perfect southern California evening. Red and orange streaks filled the sky as the sun began to set behind the ocean. Best of all, the smell of spaghetti sauce wafted from the kitchen and swirled through the evening air.

As they sat down at the table, Mr. B said, "I have a question for all of you." He paused for an instant, then asked, "Where was the Declaration of Independence signed?"

Another one of his jokes, Becky decided.

Jonathan and Charlie looked pleased, but Quinn's grouchy expression seemed to say, *Not another one of his jokes!* Worst of all, he sat right across the table from Becky.

Setting down the huge bowl of spaghetti, Mom grinned. "If no one else will try an answer, I will. Wasn't the Declaration of Independence signed in Philadelphia?"

"Very good," Mr. B said, "but it's not the answer I'm after. Come on, family, where was the Declaration of Independence signed?"

Charlie said, "If the answer isn't Philadelphia, you've got me stumped."

"Me too," Jonathan put in, suspicious.

Amanda grinned knowingly. "It was signed on the bottom."

"Right!" Mr. B answered. "Right, Amanda! You got it! How did you know that?"

"Suzanne Bennett told me," Amanda replied. "*All* of the kids know that one."

Everyone roared with laughter, and even Quinn had to smile.

Between laughs, Mr. B managed to choke out, "Seems Amanda knows how to get a laugh better than any of us."

Beaming, Amanda raised her chin importantly.

For a change, Becky didn't mind her little sister acting important. It felt good to laugh after an afternoon filled with trouble.

Still laughing, Mom said, "A happy heart does good, like medicine."

"It sure does," Mr. B agreed.

When everyone calmed down, he stroked his short gray beard seriously. His twinkling blue-gray eyes were a giveaway, though. "Ready for another one?"

"No way, these jokes are too far out of our class entirely," Charlie said with a grin.

Everyone laughed again.

Becky thought that right at this moment they seemed more like a family than they had in the entire time Mom and Mr. B had been married. "Yeah," she said to Mr. B, "I want to hear another one!"

Across the table Quinn groaned, but something in her needed to laugh wildly.

Mr. B asked, "Why does a stork stand on one leg?"

"I'll guess," Charlie said. "Because if he lifts the other leg, he'll fall down."

"Right!" Mr. B replied. "Hey, Charlie, that's very good. I can see they taught you great things in college last year."

Becky had to laugh with them, then decided to join in with a joke of her own. "What's yellow and writes?"

Mr. B replied, "A ballpoint banana! Have you been reading my joke book, Becky?"

"I haven't," she laughed, "but if I see it, maybe I will!"

She noticed that Quinn hadn't joined in the laughter. Instead, he sat eating as if the rest of them didn't exist—especially Becky Hamilton. As if she hadn't already had enough trouble today with feeling sick and having nightmares and talking about hypnotism with Cara!

———

After dinner, Becky helped clear the table. In the kitchen, Mom asked, "Are you feeling all right now, Beck?"

Becky nodded. "Cara was worried that I'd caught whatever was wrong with her Sunday morning."

Mom put a hand on her forehead. "It's possible. You do feel a little warm. Quinn told us you called to be picked up. Do you think you had a fever?"

"Maybe," Becky answered. "I sure did have bad nightmares. Skeleton hands reaching for me and bats flying at me. All kinds of scary stuff."

"Let's take your temperature. I just happen to have put our old thermometer in the cabinet with the vitamins." Mom found the thermometer, shook it down, and stuck it under Becky's tongue.

Finally she took out the thermometer and studied it. "Normal. Your temperature's normal now, Beck. Probably you should go to bed early anyhow. Thank goodness you're not baby-sitting tonight. What's on your schedule for tomorrow?"

"Nothing," Becky answered unhappily. She felt like adding, *Remember, you and Mr. B didn't want to drive me around everywhere?*

After a while, Becky said, "Bear called this afternoon."

"Oh?" Mom said. "What about?"

"He needed Lily Vanessa's phone number. One of his friends in L.A. is probably going to ask her to sing for a big youth event."

"Great," Mom said.

"I think he wanted to see how I was doing, too."

"That was nice," Mom answered. "God speaks to all kinds of people. Are you sure that the Lord didn't prompt Bear to call you?"

"Maybe," Becky decided, thinking about their conversation. Strangely enough, he'd phoned during her nightmare, right after she'd tried to scream for help.

But if it really was God who had prompted the phone call, what did He want her to do?

CHAPTER

9

Upstairs, her phone rang the instant Becky walked into her bedroom. She hurried to grab it. "Hello?"

"Hi, Beck, it's me . . . Cara."

"Hello!" Becky repeated, surprised. Wasn't Cara mad at her for explaining about hypnosis? She didn't sound mad.

"What's doing?" Becky asked.

Cara hesitated. "Now Tricia's not feeling well, and I'm feeling guiltier than ever. It's as if I started the summer flu or whatever it is that's going through the club . . . as if I've made everyone sick."

"That's crazy. You couldn't help getting sick."

Cara rushed on. "I felt fine when we rode to your slumber party and all of that night, and just felt sick on the way to church. Mom thinks it's a one-day virus. My whole family has it now. Are you better yet?"

Becky felt her forehead. Still cool. "Mom took my

temperature a while ago, and it's normal. I feel lots better since I slept this afternoon. Stop worrying about it. It's not your fault."

"Thanks," Cara replied. "Thanks a lot, Beck."

"Sure."

"I have a new problem now. I'm supposed to sit Pinky Royster tomorrow, and Tricia was going to sit Victoria Merrill and three of her five-year-old friends."

"Victoria Merrill?"

"You know, the five-year-old blond birthday girl," Cara explained. "The kids all remember us from Victoria's birthday party. Mrs. Merrill says they begged for us. Anyhow, the other TCCers are busy, and Tricia called me to see if I could do it. I told her I'd call you. . . ."

"And you want me to sit for the girls or for Pinky Royster?" Becky guessed.

"Or all of them together at Victoria's house," Cara answered. "The parents don't mind one way or another. Your mom and Mr. B wouldn't have to drive you. Mrs. Merrill would be glad to take care of transportation no matter what we decide to do."

Becky let out a long "Ufffff!"

She considered the situation. "Since you usually sit Pinky, and Tricia usually sits for the Merrill family, I'd be stuck with four five-year-old girls. I guess I'd rather do it with you, if Mom lets me go. I'll ask her." After she hung up, she decided Cara hadn't wanted to discuss hypnotism. Maybe she was even pretending it had never been mentioned during their last phone call. Well, no way would she tell Cara about hypnotism again.

From her private phone line, she phoned Mom downstairs to explain what was going on.

Minutes later, she returned Cara's call. "Mom says I can baby-sit if I go to bed early tonight, which I'm going to do."

"Great! Here's the details."

The next morning, Mrs. Merrill and little Victoria picked up Becky in their white Honda. Victoria resembled her mother closely: tan, blond curly hair, big blue eyes. Mrs. Merrill wore a white shorts outfit, and Victoria was dressed in a ruffly pink playsuit.

In the front seat, Victoria explained, "It's going to be almost like my birthday party, but without clowns and presents. Pinky Royster is coming, too!"

Becky buckled her seat belt. "Great," she said. "I love parties and I like Pinky."

Pinky was the five-year-old foster child Tricia's next-door neighbors, the Cooblers, were keeping. In fact, they were trying to adopt him. He'd been homeless and didn't talk at all until he'd astounded everyone at Victoria's birthday party last month by popping out of the clown barrel and calling out, "Happy birthday!"

Now Victoria bragged, "Pinky loves me."

"Victoria!" her mother chided.

"He does," Victoria assured them. She raised up and peered back over the top of her seat. "He really does, Becky."

Becky tried not to laugh. "That's nice, Victoria."

"Victoria, please sit down and buckle your seat belt," her mother told her.

Victoria settled back and began to do as she was told.

"Pinky's a good somersaulter."

"That he is," Becky agreed. "He may even be the world's greatest somersaulter." At Victoria's birthday party, Pinky had worn a little clown outfit and somersaulted around the yard for entertainment.

When they drove into Santa Rosita Estates, everyone was quiet. After a while Mrs. Merrill inquired, "Do you miss your old neighborhood, Becky?"

"I do," she answered. "I . . . I lived there all of my life. I just moved out about a month ago, and there aren't any kids my age in my new neighborhood. At least I haven't met any yet."

"You will when school starts," Mrs. Merrill said.

"I hope so."

"Life is full of changes," Mrs. Merrill added. "We just have to keep adjusting to change whether we want to or not. I suppose everyone tells you that."

You're right about that! Becky thought. She decided not to get into more discussion about it. Instead, she decided to trust Jesus.

As they drove past her old house, she made herself look out the window at Melanie's house on the other side of the street. One of the hardest things was being in the old neighborhood, like now.

After a while, she said, "There's Cara and Pinky standing out in Cara's driveway waiting for us."

"Looks like they're ready for fun," said Mrs. Merrill.

Becky hoped Cara wasn't secretly mad at her for the caution about hypnotism. Not that Cara had sounded mad. Instead, she'd been extremely quiet.

When they parked in Cara's driveway, Cara opened the

van's other back door. "Hi, everyone," she said with a friendly smile. "Pinky, you can get in the middle."

Pinky climbed in, silent as usual. He was a pink-faced boy with thin blond hair sticking up wildly. He wore denim bib overalls and had shoes on this morning for a change.

From the front seat, Victoria called out, "Yay, Pinky!"

Pinky grinned so widely that Becky thought he might have turned a somersault if he weren't buckling up in the backseat. Finally, he said a shy, "Hi, Victoria."

"Hi," she replied. "Hi, Pinky! Hi, Pinky! Hi, Pinky!"

"Now, Victoria, let's calm down," Mrs. Merrill said. She glanced back at Pinky. "We're glad you could come to our house this morning."

Pinky ignored her and just smiled at Victoria.

Cara murmured to Becky, "Love at first sight."

"Yeah," Becky agreed under her breath. "It still looks like it. Love for sure."

Sitting between them, Pinky grinned, and his pale blue eyes twinkled with excitement.

"You going to be good?" Cara asked him.

He nodded.

Lord, let it be a good morning, too, Becky prayed. *I've already got enough problems. . . .*

Her mind flipped through them.

First, the problem of "blending" into my new family—not to mention the aggravating Quinn.

Next, the problem of no longer being a big part of the Twelve Candles Club.

Third, the question whether Tricia is using hypnotism on the Funners for the Magic Carpet Ride.

And then there was the matter of Bear hoping they would lead

*people to Jesus. For sure and double sure, Satan didn't want them
to even consider doing anything like that!*

She sat quietly, hoping God would give her answers, but
nothing came. *Lord,* she told Him, *I put all these things in
your hands. Only you can solve all these problems.*

"What's wrong, Beck?" Cara asked her.

"Plenty," Becky answered. "That's why I was praying."

Cara's brown eyes narrowed in on hers. "You pray a lot,
don't you?"

"Not nearly as much as I should," Becky admitted. "I'd
be lots better off if I prayed more often. The Bible says we're
supposed to pray without ceasing . . . you know, pray
without stopping."

Mrs. Merrill gave her a suspicious glance in the rearview
mirror.

You'd think talking about God was dangerous, Becky
thought.

Pinky cast a glance at Becky, too, and she couldn't help
smiling at him. Thinking about God always made her happy
and feel more love for others.

"Got your frog with you today?" she asked.

He shook his head.

"God made frogs, too," Becky told him.

Mrs. Merrill must have heard her, because from the
front seat, she spoke sternly. "I don't want you talking to
Victoria and her friends about God . . . or doing any praying
around them."

Becky's heart slammed against her chest. She surely
hadn't expected such a harsh response.

"Do you understand?" Mrs. Merrill added, her blue
eyes holding Becky's in the rearview mirror.

"Yes, ma'am," Becky told her. "I understand."

"We want Victoria to make her own decisions about religion. My husband and I are most definite about that."

Becky glanced back out the window. *Another problem: a mom who doesn't want her child to hear about God!* How could anyone make a real decision if they didn't know about Jesus? What if they didn't even know the differences between religions?

Cara reassured Mrs. Merrill, "You don't have to worry about me. I don't know much about God."

"Good," Mrs. Merrill replied, her eyes on traffic. "Now let's change the subject. Victoria, why don't you do 'Pop Goes the Weasel'?"

Despite her seat belt, Victoria gave a little jump and called out a cute, "Pop!" A second later, she gave another jump and chirped, "Pop! Pop goes the weasel!"

"Pop!" Pinky called out. He gave a jump under his seat belt between Becky and Cara. "Pop goes the weasel!"

As they drove into the Merrills' house, Becky remembered yellow balloons bobbing on the mailbox the last time she'd been here. No balloons today in front of the Merrills' one-story white house. The two white pillars near the front door made the house unusual for Santa Rosita Estates, though. Actually, the pillars made the house look important . . . *self-important*, like Mrs. Merrill.

Bear always said, "People either worship God or self."

Moments after they opened the van doors, a minivan pulled up and three of Victoria's five-year-old friends tumbled out.

Seeing them, Victoria hopped straight up on the driveway and chirped an excited, "Pop!"

"Pop!" the other girls chirped, hopping straight up themselves. "Pop! Pop! Pop!"

Lord, please let us have a fun morning, Becky prayed.

"Remember," Mrs. Merrill warned her, "nothing about God."

She led them into the kitchen. "I'll be back at one o'clock. There's milk, lemonade, fruit, cookies, and tuna sandwiches in the refrigerator to serve at eleven-thirty. Everything should be cleaned up when I return."

It didn't seem like a good beginning, Becky thought. But once everyone was out in the backyard, Pinky and the girls seemed excited and kept "popping." They "popped" by themselves and, sometimes, all together, their cute little voices piping, "Pop! Pop! Pop! Pop!"

Finally, they got tired of it.

"Pinky," Victoria told him, "you somersault, like at my birthday party."

"Yeah, Pinky!" Becky cheered.

Pinky beamed, took off his shoes, and threw himself into a somersault, then another, and another. A strap from his overalls flew loose as he somersaulted around the yard, but it didn't stop him. He seemed determined to please Victoria, no matter what.

"Yay, Pinky!" everyone yelled, making him somersault in another circle.

When he quit, Victoria said, "Now let's dance the Hokey-Pokey, like at my birthday party." She gathered her friends around her on the patio. "Cindy, you stand there . . . Janie, you stand by me . . . Chelsea, you there . . . Becky and Cara, you, too!"

After singing and dancing the Hokey-Pokey, Victoria

wanted to sing songs. " 'Old MacDonald,' like at my birthday party. 'Old MacDonald.' "

She was so good at telling everyone what to do, it seemed to Becky that she and Cara weren't even needed to baby-sit.

At eleven-thirty, the two of them served lunch out on the patio table. Once everyone was seated, Victoria told Becky, "Don't pray before we eat! Don't pray!"

Becky swallowed. What was wrong with this family?

Well, no matter what they said, she was going to thank God silently for their food and ask Him to open everyone's hearts to Him.

As she started to eat, Victoria asked her, "Did you pray?"

Pinky and all four girls—Cindy, Janie, Chelsea, and Victoria—gazed at her, waiting for her to answer.

Becky decided to tell the truth. "I always try to remember to pray before I eat. I want to thank God for His blessings."

Victoria eyed her strangely.

"Aren't these tuna sandwiches delicious?" Cara put in, looking eager to change the subject.

"Delicious," Becky agreed.

She turned to Victoria. "We'll have to thank your mother for making them for us."

Victoria sighed, then began to eat. Before long, she said, "I wish it was still my birthday party and you all brought me presents. . . ."

"Would you thank us for the presents?" Becky asked her.

Victoria nodded. "I'd thank you."

Becky want to say, *That's why I thank God for my food and other blessings.*

After lunch, Becky and Cara cleaned up the table, then put everyone's drinking glasses into the dishwasher.

"Pop!" Becky chirped, giving a little jump.

"Come on!" Cara told her. "Not you, too!"

"Try it, it's fun," Becky replied and did another "Pop!"

"Pop!" Cara laughed, jumping up herself.

Becky laughed. "Pop! Pop! Pop!"

Cara laughed wildly. "Pop! Pop! Pop!"

After a moment, she said, "I didn't really know any Christian girls well until I got to know you and Tricia . . . and now Jess and Melanie, too. I didn't know being a believer could be so much fun."

"Not always," Becky answered. "But it's like Bear says . . . always an adventure. I'm afraid I thought that if I stayed close to the Lord, I would never have a bad attitude."

"You never seem to have a bad attitude," Cara objected. "For example, when you had to give up being president of the club, you recommended Melanie right away. That seemed like a good attitude to me."

"I prayed a lot about it," Becky said.

They quieted and watched the kids through the open kitchen window. Victoria was pretending to read stories to the others, but it sounded as if she had memorized them. Something about her was confused, as if she were half little girl and half mother, Becky decided. "She's peculiar."

Cara nodded. "One thing I've learned from baby-sitting this summer: Lots of little kids are weird."

"We probably were, too. Some of us are still weird."

"You know it!" Cara agreed.

"You know what?" Becky asked. "The Bible says that Christians should be a peculiar people . . . meaning 'different from others' peculiar. Different from those who don't pay attention to what He tells us in the Bible."

Cara seemed to think about it for a while, then after a moment, she asked, "How's it going with Quinn?"

Becky laughed. "Speaking of peculiar and weird!"

"I didn't mean it to seem like that," Cara said, "but it did make me think about him."

"I know," Becky answered. "I'm praying about Quinn and me someday being friends."

"I should pray like that about Paige," Cara said about her half sister. "I know I should, but I don't."

Becky decided not to say anything.

"You sure do a lot of praying," Cara remarked again.

Becky laughed. "Especially lately!"

―――――――

At one o'clock, Mrs. Merrill returned, and moments later the other girls' mothers arrived. "Did you have a good time?" they asked the kids.

Excited, the girls and Pinky "popped" all around the yard without answering.

"Appears as if they did!" laughed one of the mothers. "I'll be glad when they get over the 'popping' stage. We've taken pictures of Cindy 'popping' on video, though. Someday we'll probably enjoy seeing it again."

Finally, the other girls left, "popping" out to the cars.

Mrs. Merrill opened her purse. "Time to pay you girls and drive you home. Everyone seems happy. It looks as if you did a fine job."

Becky waited for her to ask, *Did you pray?*

But Mrs. Merrill only paid them, locked up the house, and led the way to her car.

As Becky opened the front passenger door to let Victoria in, the little girl reached up to whisper. "I wanna tell you a secret . . . a very important secret."

Becky put her head down by the girl's. "What's that?"

"I pray to God," Victoria whispered. "My nana prays for us, too. It's a secret. Don't tell. Please don't tell."

Becky gave her a hug. "I'm glad," she whispered back. "It's a wonderful secret."

"What's going on over there?" Mrs. Merrill asked as she climbed into the driver's seat.

Becky smiled at her from ear to ear, then gave a little hop and called out, "Pop!"

"It's catching!" Mrs. Merrill laughed. "Oh, I can't believe this! I suppose I'll be popping next!"

Becky climbed into the backseat. *More important, get Mrs. Merrill praying, too,* she hoped.

Thank you, Lord!

CHAPTER

10

On the way home, Mrs. Merrill drove down La Crescenta, and Becky forced herself to look at her old house again. The "For Sale" sign still stood by the street.

"SOLD!"

A red "SOLD" banner was plastered across the "For Sale" sign!

"It's sold!" she exclaimed.

She stared at the sign as if her eyes were playing tricks on her. It couldn't be true.

"I didn't want to tell you this morning," Cara said. "They didn't have 'sold' on it yet when you came to pick me up. But we heard it'd been sold."

Tears welled in Becky's eyes, and anger clenched her jaw. Something in her had hoped that her old house would never, ever sell . . . that maybe they could move back in. Some mornings when she'd awakened, she'd pretended that

Dad was still alive and living there with them.

"I'm sorry," Cara told her. "I'm really sorry. I hoped you could live here forever, too."

Becky nodded and blinked hard, staring back out the window. This was no time for anyone to see how much it hurt. Especially not Cara—not after telling how much prayer helped her . . . and what an adventure it was to be a Christian.

"It's all right," Becky said. She turned away and stared at Mrs. Merrill's blond curly hair. "I just hope nice people bought it."

But it wasn't all right. . . . Nothing about someone else buying her old house was all right!

"The new owners have two high school boys," Cara told her. "It's going to be lots different than when you and Amanda lived here."

Becky swallowed hard. "I guess so."

Two high school boys! Probably they'd ruin her room right away . . . put in footballs and sports posters. . . . Things would never be the same now that her house was really sold!

"They're moving in this weekend," Cara said, "so the boys can start school here next week."

"Great."

But there was nothing "great" about it, either. Her life had been out of control ever since Mom and Mr. B got married. She'd tried to feel at home in Mr. B's house; she'd tried hard to settle into her room there. She should never have insisted on making it like her old room because it almost felt as if it was in the wrong house. And next week, she'd have to be accepted in a new school!

Beside her, Pinky gazed at her worriedly.

"Are you okay, Beck?" Cara asked with concern.

Becky looked outside again. Mrs. Merrill was already driving up in Cara's driveway. "Sure, I'm fine. It's just sort of a shock, seeing the 'sold' sign. Probably . . . probably I'll get used to it."

Mrs. Merrill turned around. "Here we are, girls. Becky, did you want me to drive you to your house on Seaview Boulevard?"

Becky hesitated.

"Nobody's home here," Cara told her. "Why don't you stay for a while? You could go to the TCC meeting this afternoon with me. It's already going on two o'clock."

"Okay, sure," Becky answered distractedly. She realized she scarcely knew what was happening. "I'll call home."

"Thanks, Mrs. Merrill," she said. "I'll stay here."

She climbed out of the white Honda, letting Pinky out behind her.

"Thanks again, girls," Mrs. Merrill told them through her open window.

"Bye, Pinky!" Victoria shouted. "Bye, Cara and Becky!"

"Bye," Becky told them.

"Don't tell the secret, Becky!" Victoria called out as they began to back out of the driveway. "Don't tell!"

"What secret?" Cara asked.

Becky shook her head, too sad to remember.

Suddenly "the secret" hit: Victoria *prayed*, and her nana *prayed* for her. Victoria had told it just in time. *Lord, help me through this!* Becky prayed. *Please help me through this!*

"Let's walk Pinky home," Cara said. "Or would you rather go in my house and be alone?"

"I . . . I'll go along," Becky told her.

She'd have to get used to being an outsider in her old neighborhood, she told herself. She'd have to let the Lord help her get used to all of the changes in her life.

"Come on, Pinky," Cara said. "Did you have a good time this morning?"

Pinky only smiled.

Becky headed with him and Cara toward the Coobler house, where Pinky now lived—two houses from her old "SOLD" house.

As they crossed the street, she wondered if all of the neighbors were looking out and feeling sorry for her. She'd have to harden her heart, though that was the opposite of what Bear told them to do.

"Be willing to stay vulnerable," he'd told them. *"Keep your hearts tender. Don't be afraid to cry a little."*

She sure felt vulnerable now, but she didn't want to cry here in her old neighborhood. It seemed forever until they arrived at Pinky's house, and Cara rang the doorbell. Becky backed away from the front door. She didn't want to see Mrs. Coobler or to hear any kind questions she might ask.

"I'll wait out on the sidewalk," Becky said.

"Sure," Cara answered.

Pinky smiled at her, gave a jump, and called out, "Pop!"

Surprised, she managed to return a "Pop!" without hopping. Looking at him, she blinked hard and made herself smile for his sake.

Mrs. Coobler answered the door, and Pinky turned to wave at Becky. "See you!" he called out. "See you!"

"Yeah, see you!" she returned. At least he talked a little now—and she thought *she* had troubles. Pinky had been homeless not too long ago. H-o-m-e-l-e-s-s. . . ! Yep, probably she'd get used to her new house.

Before long, Cara joined her on the sidewalk. "You all right, Beck?"

"I'm all right," Becky answered, looking away. She blinked back another rush of tears.

They walked under the shade of the street trees, and she knew it was time for the complete truth.

"I'm not all right yet about moving," she told Cara, "but I've asked the Lord to help me. I can't get used to it . . . I can't accept it by myself. He's just going to have to help me get through this awfulness."

"I . . . I wish I could believe in God like you do," Cara answered. "I really wish I had lots of faith."

A sliver of hope pierced Becky's heart. She was going through trouble, but maybe God was going to use it for good for Cara.

Becky swallowed. "You can have lots of faith, Cara. You can have as much faith as anyone else because faith is just trusting in God. Trusting that He's who He says He is. You just have to accept Jesus as your Savior and Lord. It's like Bear told us last Sunday. Oops . . . you weren't there, were you?"

"No, I wasn't there."

Suddenly, Becky knew what God wanted her to ask. "Have you ever decided to give your life to Jesus?"

"I've never understood about it," Cara answered. "Worst of all, I've felt too embarrassed to tell anyone that I don't get it. Until now anyhow."

"It's nothing to be embarrassed about. Let's face it, nobody understands much about being a Christian before they become one." Approaching Cara's front steps, Becky said, "Let's sit on the steps out here, and I'll tell you whatever you want to know about it."

Cara's brown eyes shone with interest, and she sat down eagerly beside her. "Okay, tell me what I need to know now."

Where do I begin? Becky wondered.

Then she knew.

"First of all," she said, "God loves you and has a great plan for your life. That's why He gives all of us talents, like your talent for writing. Maybe you are meant to write for God's glory."

Cara nodded, still interested.

"But we're all sinful . . . you know, not perfectly holy like God, so we can't get close to Him to know His love or His plan for our lives. Still, God loved us so much that He sent Jesus to die for us so we could be close to God."

Cara spoke softly. "I don't like the idea of Jesus dying for me. That bothers me."

"I don't like to think of it, either, but He did it for love," Becky answered. "And He rose again and He's with God in heaven now. That was part of God's plan. Now, here's the hard thing to understand. When we receive Him, Jesus also lives in our hearts."

"When we receive Him?" Cara asked.

"When we ask Him into our hearts."

"I want Him in my heart, Becky."

Becky swallowed. "Then let's . . . ummm . . . bow our heads and pray."

She saw Cara bow her head, so she bowed hers, too. She

couldn't believe this was happening—and right on Cara's front steps. *Help me, Lord!*

"Just say after me," she began, remembering, "Jesus, I need You."

Cara murmured the words, "Jesus, I need you."

"Thank You for dying on the cross for my sins."

Cara repeated the words, then everything else as Becky went on. "I open my heart to receive You as my Savior and Lord . . . thank You for forgiving my sins, for giving me eternal life . . . make me what you want me to be. . . ."

All of a sudden it was over, and Becky said, "Amen."

"Amen," Cara echoed.

Becky opened her eyes and watched Cara open teary eyes. "Oh, Cara, you're a Christian now!"

Becky threw her arms around her, clumsy as it was on the front steps. "And you know what? You're my sister in Jesus now, too! We're together in the best family on earth!"

"I'm glad!" Cara choked out, hugging back.

As they sat back, Becky said, "Praise God!"

All at once her life felt wonderful. It didn't matter whether she lived in this neighborhood or not. It didn't matter whether she felt at home in her new house or not. It didn't even matter whether Quinn liked her or not, since God would give her more of His love for him—not to mention for Mr. B, Charlie, and Jonathan.

Jesus was taking care of the changes in her life by changing her heart again. He'd given her those few moments of love for Quinn during the wedding, and now she asked for that love again, and this time for help to make it everlasting. She guessed the Lord would be plenty busy improving her attitude, probably for the rest of her life!

She jumped up and felt like dancing in the warm summer air. The Lord had let her lead Cara to Him! "This is one of the best days of my life!"

"Mine too!" Cara said. "I'm so happy, I feel like I could fly!"

They both laughed as she jumped up and whirled around.

When they calmed down, Cara asked lots of questions, and it amazed Becky to realize that God had given her many of the replies. Most came from what she'd already been learning. Some of the questions, though, Bear would have to answer.

"One thing I'll always remember," Cara said as they made their way into her house. "You liked me enough to warn me about hypnosis and other un-Christian stuff being dangerous. That must have been hard to do."

"It was," Becky agreed. "Whoa! Now that we're in your house, that brings up a big question. We have to look up 'hypnosis.' "

"Look it up?"

Becky nodded. "In the dictionary."

"Where else?" Cara laughed and led the way to the bookshelves in her living room.

Becky hoped things would be all right about the Magic Carpet Ride, and that Tricia wasn't using hypnosis to make the Funners think they were whisking around to exciting places. She explained it all to Cara.

Worried, Cara opened the dictionary. She thumbed through to the end of the H's and finally found the word. She read aloud. " 'Hypnosis: a sleeplike condition psychically induced, usually by another person . . . the subject loses consciousness and responds to the hypnotist's suggestions.' "

"Thank goodness!" Becky exclaimed. "We TCCers might be wild and imaginative during the Magic Carpet Ride, but not a single Funner has ever come close to losing consciousness. There's nothing wrong with Tricia's wild imagination and using it to make fun for everyone. I'd thought about asking Bear, but now I know for sure."

"You know, I thought hypnosis might be bad even before you told me it was," Cara answered.

"Why?"

"Because Paige is always into bad stuff," Cara said about her half sister. "If something's bad, she likes it!"

———

On the way to Jess's house, the sun seemed to beam down at them more brightly than ever before. The street, houses, cars, neighborhood . . . everything shone with a joyous light.

When they arrived at Jess's outside door, they were almost floating. Jess's room had sounded noisy with voices inside, but now it was quiet.

"You knock," Cara told Becky.

"Since when do we knock at the door?" Becky inquired.

"Since today," Cara answered. "Knock."

It seemed strange, but Becky knocked on the door.

The door burst open, and there stood a big armadillo. From inside it Tricia yelled, "Surprise!"

"Surprise! Surprise, Becky!" everyone else shouted. "It's a party for you!"

Becky felt her mouth drop open. It wasn't just Jess,

Tricia, and Melanie, but Funners from Morning Fun for Kids and other kids that they'd sat for all summer. Jojo and Jimjim Davis . . . Wendy and Wanda . . . Suzanne and Bryan . . . Victoria Merrill and Pinky Royster . . . Craig Leonard, Sam Miller . . . and lots of others, including Mom and Amanda, all yelling, "Surprise!!!"

Even Bear was there.

Streamers hung from the ceiling and the parallel bars, and the kids blew noise makers, whirling and twirling all around. Somehow the TCCers had been able to keep the biggest secret of all. And she'd thought it didn't bother them much for her to give up being president!

"What's all this?" Becky asked, still amazed.

"A thank-you for being the best president the Twelve Candles Club will ever have!" Melanie replied. "Hurray for Becky!"

"Hurray!" the others shouted.

"We've been trying to keep it a secret," Tricia told her. "With Amanda around, it was almost impossible. Your mom told her on the way over here."

Amanda nodded. "That's when Mom told me. I wondered why we were bringing the armadillo outfit." Amanda ran over to Becky and put her arms out. "I love you, Becky!"

Her heart warming, Becky kneeled to hug her sister. "I love you, too!"

"There's cake and lemonade out back," Jess announced into the excitement. "Let's all head out there!"

Becky held a hand to her heart because it was beating so hard. Actually pounding. How could she ever have believed that they hadn't appreciated her?

Bear caught up with her. "I could just come by for a

minute. I'm taking Quinn out for a Coke tonight. Don't worry, God has everything in hand."

"You know it!" she whispered into his ear. "Cara just accepted the Lord!"

"Wow, praise God!" he exclaimed.

He turned to tell the others "Sorry, I have to run now!" Grinning at Becky as he left, he let loose with another excited "Praise God!"

When she looked back at the TCCers and the Funners, she tried to think of what to say to thank them for this party.

No words came, but an idea hit. She hopped and exclaimed, "Pop!" Then she popped and popped again.

"What gives with the popping?" Jess asked.

"Pop!" Becky answered, giving a hop and then spinning around with gladness. Already this afternoon, she'd had the wonder of leading Cara to the Lord, and now they'd given her this party!

Before long, all of the TCCers and Funners hopped and "popped" with her. Next summer, she'd be thirteen and probably too old for "popping," but right now it was just wacko enough to show the joy that overflowed her heart.